GROUNDSKEEPER WANTED

THE GROUNDSKEEPER TALES: 1 TO 3

COZY PARANORMAL MYSTERIES

THE GROUNDSKEEPER TALES

CEDAR SANDERSON

Copyright © 2025 by Cedar Sanderson

Stories previously published as electronic versions

The Hoodoo You Do appeared in the anthology *Haunted Library Vol 1.*

Cover Art & Design by Cedar Sanderson

Editing by Kathleen Sanderson and Liota Wakal

All rights reserved.

No part of this book may be reproduced in any form or by any electronic or mechanical means, including information storage and retrieval systems, without written permission from the author, except for the use of brief quotations in a book review.

CONTENTS

1. RAKING UP THE DEAD — 1
   - Nightfall: Clunk — 1
   - Morning Has Broken — 7
   - MicroWhatNow? — 12
   - Home Again, Home Again... — 21
   - Perchance to Dream — 27

2. THE HOODOO YOU DO — 43

3. MY GHOUL — 75
   - Jump Scare — 75
   - Don't Be a Jerk — 83
   - Traveling in Ghosts — 91
   - Denizens — 98
   - Teaching Moment — 106
   - Interview with a Ghoul — 113
   - Exploration — 120
   - Della Speaks — 128
   - Lessons — 136
   - An Unexpected Email — 140
   - Tea and Trouble — 147
   - Invisible Wounds — 155
   - Unspoken — 160

   About the Author — 169
   Also by Cedar Sanderson — 173
   You might also like... — 175

CHAPTER 1
RAKING UP THE DEAD

NIGHTFALL: CLUNK

"Psst. Hey. Chloe."

Benny, as usual, thought he was being subtle and missed it by a mile.

"What?" Chloe stopped the sort-of-golf cart next to the ghoul's chosen lair, a crumbling mausoleum. She was tired, it had been a long day, and she just wanted to go home.

The ghouls, wraiths, and ghosties had not been part of the job description. Or maybe they had, just not in so many words. The neatly printed sign next to the ornate gates had simply read: "Cemetery groundskeeper and caretaker needed. Inquire within."

Chloe had inquired. It was only after she had landed the job, moved into the tiny studio apartment, and the neighborhood cautiously accepted her that she learned she was the only serious applicant. Belleview Cemetery and Memorial Gardens might have been prime resting space a century ago. Since then, the ghetto and slums had engulfed it, and what was left of the neighborhood... The ghoul was nicer than the junkies.

"What, Benny?" She prompted when the ghoul had stood there staring into space long enough. With her luck, he'd remember what he wanted to say, and then the 'caretaker' part of her job would kick in. If he forgot, as usual, she could go home and order sushi.

"Your hair is purple." He said after a long silence. Silence was the wrong word. The cicadas were screaming into the falling darkness.

"Yes, Benny, I know." Chloe resisted the urge to reach up and touch the messy bun.

"It was green." He responded more quickly this time. He didn't make a move toward her. The one time she had touched her hair in his presence he had wanted to touch it, too. She had panicked and thrown the cart into gear to get away. Benny had sulked for a week. A sulking ghoul was surprisingly destructive. She didn't want to spark that again. So, Chloe patiently had a conversation in the twilight.

"Yes, it was. I wanted a change." It wasn't supposed to have been green. The blue dye hadn't worked as advertised.

"There's a green ghost." Benny informed her, turning his head to look down the hill. "It's lost."

"Oh." Chloe realized this, and not her hair color, was why he'd stopped her. "Um. That's... sad?"

"It cries a lot." Benny kicked the ground, looking down at his long grey toes. "Hard to sleep."

"I see." Chloe looked in the direction he'd indicated. "I'm sorry to hear that." She added politely.

Benny squinted up at her. "You could talk to it. Make it stop."

Chloe opened her mouth to protest that soothing

ghostly apparitions was not her job, then closed it again. This, too, probably fell under 'caretaker.'

"You sleep in the day." She pointed out. "Can I come back in the morning?"

He yawned, a thoroughly revolting sight, and Chloe averted her eyes.

"Didn't sleep a wink today," He informed her.

She sighed and gave up on her dreams of sushi. The delivery drivers did not come to her address after dark.

"I'll see what I can do."

She drove the cart to the next aisle and turned down the hill. Belleview, she thought sometimes, was shaped by the same rationale as taking a big bucket of paint to the top of the hill and tipping it over. The cemetery flowed down to the bottom of the hill, widening as it went, with wavy margins. In general, the lower you went, the more modern the graves. Modern being a relative term.

Chloe, who had never been terribly interested in history, had found herself intrigued by the patterns she found among the gravestones. Epidemics traceable in clustered death dates. The rise and fall of a family by the conditions of their plots. Even things as simple as naming trends caught her eye on the stones.

This section, for instance. Benny wasn't a high-class denizen of the cemetery, and the family whose mausoleum he'd occupied had died out at least fifty years ago. Chloe hadn't found any graves with the family name date later than that, anyway.

The area she was putt-putting into on her trusty ride was no longer quite as overgrown as it had been when she was hired. Which wasn't to say it was neatly manicured lawns, either. There was only so much Chloe could do on her own, and a hesitant question to her boss about bringing in a crew... He had lowered the newspaper slightly, fixing her with one laser-bright blue eye while the bushy gray eyebrow inched up his forehead like a strange caterpillar.

"If you can find workers, by all means." The newspaper - and Chloe wondered where he got them daily, as the last paper in the city had gone out of business months ago - rose again like a door closing. Chloe had retreated to her little desk.

Her feeling of victory hadn't lasted, and it felt like sour frustration now, a month later as she inched past the brush hiding gravestones. She had to consciously unclench her jaw. No-one had responded to her ad for men willing to do work in the cemetery.

It had gotten very dark in this part of the graveyard, with the tall old trees and the brush that arched over the access path. Chloe had been given the cart to use, as a truck would have been useless in much of the cemetery. She was grateful. No one had asked to see her driver's license, which was good as she hadn't gotten one. Yet.

She switched on the feeble little headlights, and a pair of startled glowing eyes resolved themselves into an opossum who quivered, torn between playing dead and running away. He rolled over, paws up.

"Drama-llama." Chloe muttered, stopping the cart. She had no intention of running the wee beast over. She got out of the cart and made her way to the front of it.

The tunnel of brush narrowed ahead, and Chloe hesitated, ignoring the possum who had given up his ploy and was hustling away through the shadows. She couldn't hear anything out of place.

Her first ghost encounter, a week after starting this job, had scared her stiff for about two minutes. You couldn't be afraid of a big frowsy woman whose glowing hair made a fluffy halo around her indefinite face. Especially not when she marched up, put her hands on her hips, bent forward slowly and deliberately toward the girl standing there petrified with fear and said, "Boo."

Chloe had been frozen, her blood cold as ice, right up until that second. It surprised both of them when what had popped out of her mouth was: "Boo Who?"

She had no idea how it worked, but the apparition had laughed so hard that she exploded into a million shimmering bits. It was like standing inside a firework for just a second. Then the ghost was gone, and Chloe was alone again, and no longer afraid.

After that encounter, the other inhabitants of Belleville slowly began to reveal themselves. Chloe was sure she still hadn't met all of them. Like this lost ghost she was looking for. She turned around, looking into the dark.

Out of the corner of her eye, she caught a flicker of movement. Chloe stopped turning and pretended to look in the other direction. The ghost gathered, like fog coming together in a semi-solid and faintly luminous shape. Chloe didn't dare look right at it, or move, lest she scare it away. The ghost flitted around like it was nervous. It was soundless.

Chloe stood there, and then her stomach growled loudly. The ghost jerked away, brightening. Chloe turned her head, reflexively.

"Sorry!" She blurted out before she thought it through.

The ghost dimmed, wavered. Chloe held out a hand. "Don't go! I wanted to talk to you."

The apparition grew brighter again, and for the first time Chloe could make out proper shapes and features. They didn't help her much. The pale oval face with the sharply pointed chin looked like a child's, neither male nor female. The eyes were dark shadows in the glow.

"Hello." Chloe said for lack of a better idea.

It drew a little closer, then paused. She got the impression that it wanted to bolt, but for some reason it also wanted to communicate.

"I'm Chloe, the caretaker. Can I help you?" She mentally cursed her retail-trained reflexes. What was she going to do for a ghost?

That seemed to help, though. The ghost didn't get brighter, it got more solid. Not corporeal, but she couldn't see right through it any more. It was dressed in an old-fashioned shirt, trousers, and a pair of suspenders. The haircut was what made her think it must have been a boy. Chloe waited. She had discovered that the dead were slow. It was like they no longer had any sense of the passage of time.

"You found me." It wasn't so much a sound, as a suggestion of a voice.

"I did." Chloe agreed. "Benny pointed me at you."

"I'm lost."

"Well, it's a bit messy in this area." Chloe looked toward the cart, where the headlights were still lighting up the path. "You have been crying."

"I'm so alone," he said. "So alone and I can't find my way home."

"Then let's get you back to your place." Chloe suggested. She had no idea if that would work. Would it work? Reconnecting ghost and grave? It seemed like an idea. A place to start.

The ghost looked around, its face moving while the body did not. One pale slender hand reached out toward her. Chloe shuddered as the head made a full revolution before the eyes were aimed at her again. "I can't remember..."

"Can't remember what?" Chloe tried to be patient. "Where your grave is?"

"Can't," cried the ghost, seeming to clutch at its face. The soft voice rose to a howl. "Remember! Anything!"

Chloe suppressed her first reaction, which was to call the ghost, like the possum, a drama-llama. She'd probably have to explain what a llama was. "I'll tell you what. If you'll lurk here quietly, I'll come tomorrow and we can look together."

The ghost stopped with a faint sobbing gasp. "You'll help?"

"Only if you are quiet." Chloe felt like she was trading off Benny for the ghost as problems went. The ghost smelled better, though.

"Yes. Yesterday was… I don't remember yesterday." The ghost started to fade.

Chloe hopped into her cart and said, firmly: "tomorrow at dusk."

She backed up carefully. Turning around was not possible here, and she wasn't certain where this path came out, or if it did. Some of them dead-ended. The ghost had gone, and she was able to get home with no more interruptions.

MORNING HAS BROKEN

Morning got off to a great start.

"Horace. Stop being lewd with the mermaid." Chloe had caught the movement out of the corner of her eye but deliberately didn't look in that direction. She didn't want to see.

There was a splash, then a spray of water hit her in the face. She tightened her hands on the grips of the zero-turn mower and debated just moving on with her work. But no... caretaker. She brought the machine to a stop and turned to look at the Merman. Nymph, although she thought that was female, and Horace was definitely not. Fortunately, he was discreetly fishy and finned from an appropriate level below the belly button.

Chloe didn't want to talk to Horace. She had work to do. Part of why she had wanted this job was that she liked mowing - and the zero-turn was fun to use. Plus, she wanted to have time today to scout out the ghost's path to see if she could navigate it without having to back up all the way out.

Horace, Chloe thought to herself while trying not to laugh at her own joke, was a wet blanket. He was currently sitting on the edge of the fountain, dripping. His pale, clammy skin had a distinctly green color to it. His tail, which was mostly still in the water, was a muddy green color, a little darker than the water. She wasn't sure of the color of his hair - she had never seen it dry. It was straggling all down his face onto his shoulders, looking black.

"Why won't you come with me?" Horace was asking now. "My city beneath the waves is wondrous beyond compare!"

He stretched out one long, skinny hand toward her. Chloe leaned on the handlebars of her mower with her elbows and counted down raised fingers with her other hand. "One, I breathe air. Two, I'm not convinced there is a city. Three, I'm working. Four, I don't want a boyfriend. And finally," she made a fist and shook it at him, laughing. "You'd eat me!"

He laughed, too. Horace, she had discovered after her

initial impression of him as a creepy slimeball, wasn't quite as awful as he tried to be. There was a reason, she suspected, that he lived in an algae-infested fountain in the nearly-deserted (by humans) cemetery.

"A guy can try, can't he?" Horace splashed his fins, but this time aimed the spray away from her.

"Yes, but when a girl says no, you gotta respect that." Chloe admonished him. "You'll never get a girl if you don't respect her. How is Goldie?"

The change of subject worked. Horace broke into a huge grin, which would have been better if it hadn't revealed how sharklike his teeth were. Right down to the multiple rows and shedding. Chloe suppressed a shudder. She hated it when normals called her weird and avoided her, so from the beginning she had decided her new community here in the cemetery would get care, not fear, from her.

"Goldie is getting fat!" Horace dove back into the fountain and reappeared a second later, cupping a huge koi carefully in his hands. He showed Chloe, then released his pet. "Isn't she a chonk? Such a beautiful chonky gurl!"

"Yes, she is. Let me know if you need more special food for her." Chloe restarted the mower.

"We're good!" Horace shouted over the roar of the engine. With a wave, he dove and disappeared into the murky waters.

Chloe rotated her machine and went back to work once she'd punched up her playlist again. The big headphones had been expensive, but totally worth it. Once she got into the groove with the mowing, she could just zone and chill. It was the best job. It was the other aspects of her job that were a little more challenging. But honestly, ghouls, ghosts, and other creeps were still better than McCampbell's managers had been. That, and she didn't have to talk to humans in this job. Much.

She knocked off the mowing when she had done the quadrant she'd designated for the day, and headed toward the path where she'd met the lost ghost the night before. Benny's home, which was a miniature greek temple replica, was closed up tight. He was probably sleeping. She hoped he was, anyway. Cranky ghouls were not a pleasant part of the job.

The path was less scary in the daylight, but still a green tunnel of brush. She frowned at it, sitting in her cart with the engine idling before she decided whether to walk it or drive. Sighing, she shut off the engine and walked. Backing was not her strong suit. Learning to drive had been a massive PITA, and if her parents hadn't insisted that she learn to drive before she moved out, then she would have skipped it. She could take the bus! She had said.

Then you have to rely on the bus schedule, her mother had told her. It wasn't until Chloe had to use the bus for a year that she really understood why being able to drive herself was important. Still... she didn't like driving. The cart was ok. The cart didn't make her feel like she was hurtling down the road atop tons of lethal steel. That was scary.

There was no sign of the ghost, but Chloe had already learned that she wouldn't see them in daytime. Hear, yes, sometimes. But the visible seemed to require darkness. Right now, the sun was up and cheerful light flooded the tunnel, filtered through the leaves to make everything look green. Like being underwater. She wondered if this is what it would look like in Horace's city. She'd never know, because if she took him up on it, she'd be dead, too.

The path did go all the way through, although a bit

weedy towards the end where it reconnected with one of the many roads that wound a maze-like pattern through Belleview. She walked out onto it, and looked back. If she didn't know she'd just been through there, she wouldn't have realized there was a path. Well, she'd bring the cart through today and tomorrow, then come back with the brush hog. That was scarier than the lawnmower, but... Chloe squared her shoulders. Her boss had said he trusted her to make headway on what had once been a wonderful monument to those who had passed.

Sometimes she wondered if he knew just how many hadn't passed on. That there was a thriving and diverse community here in Belleview. She waded back into the weeds, looking carefully at the ground. No headstones. This was a maintenance path, then, just a neglected one. Wouldn't be the first she'd found, nor likely the last.

Chloe returned at twilight, having taken a lesson from the day before and gotten her sushi early. She drove confidently down the path she'd scouted, her dim headlights giving her just enough light to be sure she wasn't going to run over the opossum... but she drove halfway into the ghost.

She almost screamed when he suddenly appeared and she couldn't stop in time.

"Are you all right?" She threw it into park and jumped out. "Oh my gosh, you can't wander out in front of people like that."

"Oh." He looked down vaguely where his middle disappeared into the golf cart's short hood. "I don't feel that." He took a few steps and popped out of the entanglement.

"Right." Chloe took a deep breath and tried to calm her jangled nerves. Of course, he didn't. "So. Have you remembered anything?"

He brightened, literally. "I remember many things. I stayed awake and thought until you came, so I could tell you!"

"So where is your grave?"

"I don't know. I know my name, though! And my parent's names…"

She pulled her little notebook out of her pocket. "I have an idea."

MICROWHATNOW?

Chloe's interview with the ghost was not entirely satisfactory. She was able to get his name, Bartholomew Parloa, and the names of his parents, his own parent's dates of death, and his birthday, but he was a little fuzzy on his own date of death. Armed with this information and as much as she could figure out about his life, which seemed to her to have been the very utmost in boring, Chloe headed for her next destination.

This was a new facet in the caretaker part of her job. It just seemed to grow more complex all the time: Investigator. A very private investigator, of course.

The big city library was quiet as a tomb (or at least, one that wasn't at Belleview and housing an entire family) when she walked in the next morning. She looked around the echoing lobby with its ornate columns and statuary. This was a very different place than the libraries she had grown up with. This one was more like a museum.

The other thing was that she had no idea where to start looking for records of people who had lived and died in the city. She wasn't even sure she was in the right place. But her mother had taught her that when in doubt, start with the library. Chloe's next idea was to find a librarian.

There didn't seem to be anyone sitting at the main desk, so Chloe wandered into one of the side rooms. She disturbed a slumbering cat, who put his ears forward and started to walk towards her. He stopped to stretch and yawn, and a pair of slender bone-white hands scooped him up by the middle.

"Can I help you?"

She was a rather old-fashioned looking lady, the very ideal of a librarian. Dressed in a long black skirt and a black blouse, with a chunky white cardigan that looked homemade, she had a pair of glasses with no ear pieces that dangled from a chain on her chest. Her long white hair was pulled back into a tidy bun, unlike Chloe's sloppy, spiky purple one. Chloe found herself a little self-conscious suddenly, standing there in a hoodie and jeans.

"Uh, I'm looking for... somebody. Well, ok, I'm looking for something about him. He's dead."

The woman raised her eyebrow slightly. "I see."

"Er, um, it's genealogy!" Chloe grasped at straws. "It's an, um, ancestor. I'm trying to find his grave."

"Have you visited findagrave dot com?" The woman asked.

Chloe blinked. She hadn't expected such technological savvy from a librarian who could have walked out of that musical her mother loved. She looked very old school.

"Well, I'm pretty sure he's in Belleview, and that's not fully mapped yet."

"Oh. Oh, I see... Belleview. Perhaps I can help. Let me show you where birth and death records are kept. They are in microfiche, have you ever used that?"

"Uh, no." Chloe admitted.

"I can show you how. It's not complicated, just a little tedious. If you have a date of death, that would be helpful."

"Ah, er, I'm a little fuzzy on that. Date of birth, yes. And well, I've got his parent's dates of death."

"Ah, excellent. We should be able to narrow it down, then." The librarian led Chloe through a door that did not look like it was normally used for public access, and then down a long dark hallway lit by dim sodium bulbs. They shed a slightly yellow glow onto the whole scene, and added to the growing feeling of unreality Chloe was feeling.

The woman still held the cat, who dangled limp as a scarf from her hands.

"Is the cat all right?" Chloe finally asked.

"Esmeralda is a ragdoll," the librarian explained. "She relaxes when picked up." She added drily, "It is not a survival trait."

They came to a door, having gone down a short flight of metal stairs. The librarian transferred Esmeralda to the crook of her arm and unlocked the door. The room inside was dim, and she said over her shoulder to Chloe, "The lights take a minute," as she pushed up the switch.

Chloe could hear them as they came on, with an odd buzzing and clicking. They illuminated a huge room full of large metal racks. On the racks were innumerable boxes, all neatly labeled.

"Here you go," The librarian directed Chloe's attention to the desks lining one wall, starting at the door. They were separated by partial dividers, and each station held a positively archaic metal apparatus.

"This is a microfiche reader." She put Esmeralda down on the swivel chair seat. The cat promptly hopped down and walked deliberately away from both of them, her tail aloft like a smoky plume.

Chloe looked in the direction the cat was headed, and saw the ghost. The librarian was still talking, so after one wide-eyed glance at the slender translucent man dressed in old-fashioned clothes, she looked resolutely away again.

A short lesson in how to load the microfiche reader later, Chloe followed her new library guide into the racks. To her relief, the ghost was nowhere in sight. The librarian had produced a notepad and pencils from the desk's single drawer and had written the names and dates on it.

"I'll show you how to find the first, then I'm afraid you're on your own." She pointed. "Dates." There was a placard at the end of each rack, Chloe saw. It bore a date range. "Then smaller ranges by box. You cannot remove anything from the room," she added.

"Oh, yes, of course not." Chloe flushed. She hadn't even considered it, but it felt awkward to be reminded.

"We don't allow patrons down here, but we are so short-staffed..." The librarian tut-tutted and lifted her glasses, which pinched onto the bridge of her nose. She peered through them at the label on the box. "November 2 to November 28. Not quite."

Chloe looked at the next box. "November 29 to December 20?"

"Sounds right. Can you manage that?"

Chloe could, although as she followed the woman back toward the desks, she considered that this could be a workout if she had to go through many boxes.

The ghost appeared in the periphery of her vision. He was standing on the other side of the racks looking through a gap where boxes had been removed. He was the most well-defined ghost Chloe had ever seen, but she couldn't tell what color his eyes had been as they locked gazes. He smiled with a friendly nod, and Chloe tried not to trip in her surprise. Spilling that box would be a hot mess.

The lady librarian pointed at one of the long tables

between the racks and desks. "Put that there... oh, Kung! How did you get in here?"

Kung, it seemed, was a very large and muscular black cat, almost a half-scale panther, Chloe thought. He was sitting on the chair looking at them, his ears pricked. Esmeralda was curled up on the cushion of the chair next to his.

Chloe put the heavy box down on the table and offered him her knuckles to sniff. He politely whiffed, then stropped her hand with the side of his face, his long whiskers tickling her forearm.

And just like that, the librarian was gone, leaving the door ajar behind her.

Chloe looked after her. "I never even got her name." She muttered aloud.

From behind her, a voice responded calmly, "Her name is Penelope. Penny White." Chloe turned around and the ghost smiled disarmingly at her. "My name's Mark," He said. "Mark Long, pleased to meet you." He stuck out a hand and she looked from it to him. Then tentatively reached out her hand towards him. She wasn't quite sure what to expect. So, she was both surprised, and not surprised when, rather than being able to close her hand on his, her hand just sort of passed right through his with kind of a cool tingling sensation.

"I'm Chloe," She said. "Chloe Brandt."

"Nice to make your acquaintance!" He was the most cheerful ghost she'd ever met.

"And, er, yours." Chloe answered. "So is this where you, um..."

"Oh, I don't live here." Mark said. "This just was my favorite place when I was alive and now that I'm dead I have all the time on my hands to be able to do the projects that I wanted to get done before... Well, you know."

"Oh, I see."

She looked at the box on the table behind him, "I, er, am working on a project myself."

"I heard that," Mark said. "So, this guy you're looking for is..." He walked over to the box and pulled the lid off. Chloe was startled. If he hadn't been able to take her hand, how could he handle the box lid? He started flipping through files. Chloe realized as she watched his fingers in the file that his movements were not in synchronicity. He was moving things by some other means than physical manipulation. Which didn't reassure her exactly. The big black cat jumped up on the table again. He didn't even look at the cat.

"Kung, get down. You know you're not supposed to be up here."

The cat tilted his nose upward as if he were offended at the very thought. Chloe stifled a giggle. Esmeralda, who had been curled up on one of the seats in the chairs under the table poked her head up above the table and saw Mark. She hopped up on the table and walked over towards the apparition and tried to lean on his arm. She fell right through with a somewhat foolish look on her face. He laughed.

"Kung knows better." He said over his shoulder to Chloe, "but Esmeralda still hasn't gotten used to the idea that I'm not a real person. She's a lovely pussy but she's a bit dim."

Chloe decided to ignore the ghost part of the equation and take advantage of Mark's being willing to help her. She walked up to stand by his elbow and peer into the box of the files.

"What are these? I was expecting, er, well... records."

"Newspaper files," He said. "Given the date range, any births and deaths would've been reported in the newspaper. Back in the day, that's how we did it." He came up to the December section and started slowing down a little bit. His rapid manipulation flicked through the files faster than Chloe could read along. He stopped and pulled out a piece of plastic looking stuff.

"This is what you're looking for." He stuck the file up sideways so they could find where it had gone and handed the object to her, warning "Don't touch the surface of it, just handle it by the edges, okay? I'll show you how to get it in the reader."

She turned and went back to the reader that Penny had so kindly switched on for her. "Slot it in right there..." Mark pointed. "And then here, turn on the lamp..." he pointed again.

"How can you manipulate the files, but not the switches?" Chloe asked, feeling confused.

He grinned, "Clever of you to notice that. I think it's the electricity. It interferes with my field."

Chloe stared at him, fascinated. This was the first time she met a ghost that had some awareness of their abilities beyond just simply dead or alive or, well - she thought back to the blousy woman at Belleview -making a joke. But then again this was the longest she'd had a conversation with the ghost as well, other than Bartholomew, and that wouldn't really count as a conversation. More like an interrogation to try and get something useful out of the distraught youth. The plastic - or celluloid, as Mark said it was - with the lamp shining through it threw a greatly enlarged replica of the text onto the screen. Which she could read and flip through by manipulating buttons, from page to page. Somewhat to her chagrin, the microfiche contained in miniature a complete replica of the entire newspaper, not just the section that she wanted.

With Mark over her shoulder helping her navigate - because it turned out that the Cincinnati Enquirer had a pattern in how it laid out its paper - she was able to quickly flip through. He had her slow down when she got close enough to the destination to find listings of deaths, then births. There were more deaths than there were births, it looked like. At least to her quick eye, looking for patterns. She found herself intrigued with the idea of coming back here to research some of the other inhabitants of the old cemetery. There had been some interesting names she'd spotted during her cleaning.

She turned her head and looked at Mark. "So, I have a question you might not be able to answer."

He raised his eyebrows and grinned. "Try me! I'm the ultimate research librarian." He replied archly.

Chloe grinned back at him. He might be dead, but she liked him. "I'm guessing this isn't someplace that they just let the GP wander into..."

"GP?" He interrupted.

"General public. I'm just a random person off the street."

He blinked. "Have you looked at yourself in the mirror?"

"Huh?" Chloe wasn't sure what he was talking about, and he gestured towards her chest. She looked down obediently and realized that she was wearing a hoodie that her boss had supplied. A sort of a working uniform, along with several T-shirts. Emblazoned across the front in the ornate curlicue font used on the gates was 'Belleview.'

"Oh... but how did Penny know..."

"Well, I'm guessing she had a conversation with your employer."

Chloe blinked again. She wasn't sure when, when she'd only told her boss that morning. He did have a telephone on his desk, a very old one and very heavy. Chloe used it once, but she had never seen him use it and it seemed out of character for him. She supposed he would've had time to pick it up and dial when she had left and was working her way towards the library on the bus. That was not a quick trip.

"Oh, I think I see?" It also meant that her boss would've deduced what she was doing other than just that she had told him that she needed to do some research. Work related. He had nodded at her over his newspaper. Newspaper. She looked down at the microfiche.

"I think there's more going on here than I realized."

Mark nodded. "Clever girl, keep going, you'll figure it out."

Chloe flipped over another page and pointed, "Look, there he is. Bartholomew Parloa, born December 18, 1895 to parents John and Ella. This doesn't really help me find his grave."

"I think you might be better served to try with his parents. If you can find their graves, chances are he's buried near them. At least if you're looking at Belleview. It seems likely that it would be a family plot."

"Would there be a picture of their gravestones in the newspaper?"

He shrugged, "That seems unlikely. You'll notice that there's not a lot of photographs in the newspaper of this era."

"Point," Chloe admitted, "let's put this back."

"I'll help you find their deaths."

HOME AGAIN, HOME AGAIN...

A couple of hours later, Chloe left the library, having made a new friend and having been reassured that she was welcome to come back anytime. Before leaving she found Esmeralda for final pats. Kung had disappeared somewhere back into the stacks during their efforts. He had appeared a couple of times while they were looking for boxes. Once on the top of the stacks with his chin hanging down and his big golden eyes staring at Chloe.

Mark had pspsps'd at him, telling him to go away and stop trying to scare the girl. Chloe laughed. "He's not going to scare me. He's a big old tomcat, isn't he now?" She said that last in a syrupy tone she reserved for babies and animals.

Kung had blinked slowly and put his head on one side.

Mark had commented, "He doesn't usually like people. Er, living persons."

Chloe, sitting on the bus, clutching her notepad with the information that she hoped would help get her closer to finding Bartholomew's grave, thought about this. She could see ghosts and talk to them. Strange cats liked her. What was she?

When she arrived back in Belleview. Chloe stood for a second, hesitating in the circular driveway that led up to the grand house of the man who was her boss. He seemed to be in charge of the cemetery; she had never gotten a title from him. She turned, instead of going towards the stables where the lawncare equipment was kept. She went inside to the room that looked a lot like the library and he called their office. The house was still, dark, and quiet as it usually was.

Chloe wasn't sure that anyone else but him lived here. At least no one that she had seen, and she had never seen him outside of their office. He was always there when she came in the morning, sipping a cup of tea from an elegant teacup, a full tea service on the table and reading his newspaper. He'd been quite delighted when she joined him for tea, commenting that most young people didn't have a taste for it these days.

Now, it was afternoon, a time that Chloe wasn't usually in the office and she wasn't even sure she would find him, but she did. He was sitting with his back to the door at his own desk, much more majestic affair than her own, with a rolltop he could pull down to conceal the myriad of pigeonholes stuffed full of papers. He was writing with a gold fountain pen. He didn't look up when she came in and she stood quietly and waited for him to notice her and speak. It seemed rude to interrupt his thoughts. After a moment he put the pen down and looked up at her with a faint smile on his pale face.

"Good afternoon, Chloe."

"Good afternoon sir."

"Was your trip to the library productive?" He asked.

So, he had known exactly where she had gone, and what she was doing. Well, he had known where she was going anyway.

"I don't know yet, Sir." She looked down at the notebook in her hands. "I'm trying to find..." she looked up at him. "I'm not going crazy, Sir."

"Ah." He raised both his eyebrows. "Is that what you're worried about?"

"Well," She took a deep breath. "There's a ghost..."

He nodded, "would you perhaps like some tea with cookies?"

Chloe blinked. That wasn't the reaction she had been expecting to her announcement.

"Yes, please?" Cookies sounded really good and she did like the way he made his tea.

"Then I think it is time for you to meet the rest of my household." He lifted his hands and clapped twice sharply. The sound echoed through the room. In the hallway brisk footsteps sounded.

The door to the office - the other door, the one Chloe never used - opened.

"Ah, Della! Tea for two, please."

The skeleton in the Victorian dress moved her head, directing her empty eye sockets from Chloe's boss to Chloe and back again.

"Shall I introduce you? I suppose it's time." Mr. Cruor smiled, his thin lips nearly disappearing.

"Della Dear, this is Chloe Brandt. Chloe, this is Miss Dear. She has been here... well. Longer than I have."

Chloe wasn't sure what the etiquette books said about being formally introduced to a skeleton.

"Hi? Nice to meet you."

The skeletal woman inclined her head, jaw bone almost touching the floral brooch pinned at the base of her throat to the lace collar of her dress. Then she withdrew and the door closed behind her.

"Good, good." Mr. Cruor rubbed his hands together. "She likes you."

"How can you tell?" Chloe blurted.

"She acknowledged your existence. You'd be surprised what people can persuade themselves doesn't exist if they ignore it hard enough."

Chloe wasn't sure how this translated to liking, but she let it slide.

"About the ghost, sir."

Mr. Cruor gestured at the chairs by the table. "Please, sit."

Once she had taken her place, and he seated himself on the opposite side of the small table, he asked, "Now, which ghost?"

"He says his name is Bartholomew Parloa. He was bothering Benny."

Mr. Cruor raised both his eyebrows and his lips tucked in at the corners, like he was hiding a smile. "You have met Benny."

"Er." Chloe realized she shouldn't have mentioned the ghoul. But after meeting the skeleton… "I'm not crazy."

"Indeed, you are not. Benny would be hard to imagine." Her boss looked up, just before the door opened. Della came in, appearing to glide over the smooth floor with her long skirt almost touching it. Chloe had no idea how Mr. Cruor had heard her coming, she floated rather than clattered as she moved. Chloe wondered how she stayed together. As Della set the tea tray smoothly on the table, Chloe could see that she was made up of polished white bones, no connective tissue in sight, or wires.

"Tea?" Mr. Cruor poised the pot over one of the flowered cups.

"Yes, please." Chloe waited until he had poured and handed her a cup and saucer. That was followed by a small plate piled with crustless sandwiches and cookies.

"This looks… beautiful." She told him. For the second time that day she felt conscious that she was dressed appropriately for mowing lawns. Not High Tea, or whatever this was.

"I told you she liked you." He was making that 'not-smiling' face again. "So, you know Benny, and more than one ghost. Doubtless other members of our community as well."

Chloe, caught with her mouth full of sandwich, just nodded.

He kept talking. "Which means this ghost is somehow special, since you have not previously ventured to break your silence. As he was bothering Benny, and I can't imagine even someone as kind-hearted as yourself being entirely altruistic over the ghoul..."

Chloe felt her cheeks get warm with a blush. She really had been motivated more by a desire to shut Benny up.

"Just what is extraordinary about this ghost?"

"He's lost," Chloe explained. "He is pretty young. He was able to tell me when he was born, and his name, but that was only after I got him to calm down. He was crying. Loudly." She added to explain Benny's involvement.

"I see. The intent of the trip to the library was to take him home once you had an address?"

Chloe shook her head. "I want to find his grave, first, and see if that, er, works." She really wasn't sure what it would take to lay a ghost to rest. This just seemed like a good place to start.

"I see."

When he didn't say anything else, Chloe started to explain herself.

"So that area, where I found him, is pretty overgrown. And he can't remember when he died. But I thought if I could look up more about his family, I might be able to find his plot."

Mr. Cruor's eyebrows went up a little in what Chloe was interpreting as surprise.

"I found his parent's obituaries," She kept talking after a sip of tea. "And his. Turns out they all died in the same week after an accident. He didn't know anything about his death, but he remembered theirs, which was weird." Chloe subsided into silence and another cookie.

Her boss cleared his throat. "Why didn't you come to me? I have a very good map of Belleview."

Chloe felt a surge of mingled relief and frustration. "I thought... I was afraid you'd think I was crazy. And fire me." She had started loud, then her voice faded out as she finished up.

The lines of his face softened a little. "You like your job here at Belleview?"

"I do." Chloe looked into her teacup, at the little pieces of leaves dark against the china through the amber liquid. "It's... not what I expected. The caretaker part, I mean."

"Oh?"

She looked at him through her eyelashes. He was sipping tea and looking at her with those light gray eyes. But not judging, she thought.

"I mean, I thought it was going to be like taking care of a garden. With sculptures, sort of. But there are people, and they need things too, and they can't exactly leave this place, so..." She shrugged and lifted her chin. "I take care. It's in the job description."

He smiled, a warm and gentle expression that lit up his face. "I think when I hired you, I may have made the best decision in my long life. You are a rare jewel, Miss Brandt."

Chloe didn't know what to say to that. She opened her mouth, and all that came out was: "eep?"

"Now. Let us see if we can properly locate this lost soul of yours." He clapped, a single clap this time, and the footsteps in the hall were different. Heavier, Chloe thought.

She wondered who, or what, would come through the door.

PERCHANCE TO DREAM

The door opened and a huge head and shoulder appeared. "Yeth, Mathter?"

The face of whatever that was fascinated Chloe. It was gray-green… was that a fern growing in his eyebrow… ridge… formation over the deepset eye? The mouth, nose, and eyes were all more like cracks in slightly wet-looking skin than they were fully shaped and recognizable. The head was mostly bald, and what there was growing on it looked more like moss than hair. Plus, he had to be at least eight feet tall. Those doors were seven feet if not more, and he was stooping just to look in on them.

"Trunk, I wanted to introduce you to Miss Brandt." Mr. Cruor had stood and was heading toward his desk.

The enormous… being swiveled his head as much as he could. "Pleasmeetcha."

"Pleased to meet you too, Trunk." Chloe responded, feeling like she was in shock.

"I need the maps from… When did you say, Miss Brandt?"

Chloe wondered why he was being so formal, but followed his lead. "The deaths were in 1912, Mr. Cruor."

"So I think the last map before the Great War, then." He pulled a key ring with a single large skeleton key out of a cubbyhole, and walked toward Trunk.

"Herkay." The head retreated and was replaced with a massive hand. The key looked like a toy as Mr. Cruor placed it on his palm. Then that, too, was gone and the door was closing in his wake. Chloe was no longer surprised she could hear him walking. She was more surprised the floors held him.

"Trunk," Mr. Cruor returned to the table and set tea things on the tray. Chloe followed suit. "Is a troll. Specifically, the species of troll bound to bridges. You have read about them."

"I didn't think they were real, though." Chloe said.

"Oh, very real. Very shy, and displaced from their habitats in many areas, with the result that they are endangered." Mr. Cruor shook his head, frowning. "I am afraid Trunk may be the last of his kind on the Ohio River."

"He lives under a bridge?" Chloe knew they weren't far from the big river - one of her favorite things as a girl had been to go to the overlook park and watch the ships traveling up and down.

"He did, and now he lives here in Belleview. There are some small bridges, and that suffices for him, but his heart yearns for something bigger."

"Oh. That's..." Chloe realized she felt bad for the huge creature. "That's really sad."

"You are familiar with host plants?" Her boss asked, taking the tea tray to the small table near the inner door.

"Like Monarch butterflies needing milkweed plants?" Chloe was wondering what he was talking about now. Her day thus far had been... Unsettling.

"Precisely so. Trunk's kind needs bridges."

Chloe had a wild mental image of Trunk hatching out into something with wings. Really, really big wings. She felt a giggle starting and tried to change the subject.

"This means my research at the library wasn't necessary?" She asked.

"No, no, it was vital." He cocked his head. "Ah, there he

is. Such a gifted organizer, Trunk is. The archives were hopeless before his arrival."

Chloe wanted to ask when that had been, but that would lead toward knowing Mr. Cruor's age, and she had decided some time ago she didn't want to know. Knowing too much was...

She realized what she had done. "You needed the dates."

"Yes, they help with finding the proper map. You see, they have changed so, over the years, and the cartographers have not always consulted the previous work."

"Findagrave doesn't have all the cemetery mapped." Chloe commented, remembering the librarian - Penny's - question.

"No... I'm afraid it was impossible to let them continue." Her boss looked upset, briefly, before his usual calm returned.

"I understand." Chloe did see it, now, that letting random people wander all over Belleview, poking into the brush and hidden places... "That could be very..."

"Inconvenient." Her boss said firmly, opening the door. A rolled-up piece of paper half as long as he was tall was thrust inside. "Thank you, Trunk. Efficient as ever."

There was a noise that sounded pleased to Chloe, and the door closed again. Mr. Cruor's smile had returned as he walked briskly toward the table where they had been having tea shortly before. Chloe thought to herself that he didn't move like an old person, even if his hair was thin and white. He unrolled the big map on the table. Chloe grabbed a couple of things from her own desk to keep the corners from rolling up again.

This was supposed to be just about finding Bartholomew's grave, but Chloe was excited that she would finally get a birds-eye view of the whole of her workplace. She bent over the table, looking at the age-faded markings on the map.

"This looks…" She didn't look up as she spoke.

"All hand drawn, of course." He put a magnifying glass down in front of her. "I recommend this."

"Thank you." Chloe felt very much like a detective, holding the magnifying glass and peering at the tiny writing. "It's written so small!"

Her boss, on the other side of the table, where he seemed to be having no trouble at all reading upside-down, murmured agreement.

"Did you say Parloa?" He asked a minute later.

"Yes." Chloe looked up, hopeful. "P-a-r-l-o-a."

"Ah! you can spell when you want to." He flashed a laughing look at her. "False alarm, I'm afraid, this is a Barlow with a crabbed hand."

Chloe didn't want to ask what that was. Now she was going to dream about giant crabs roaming the cemetery. She kept looking. Behind them, the door opened, and Chloe looked around to see Della quietly taking the tea tray away. After that distraction, she was trying to find her place again.

"Oh!" Chloe almost squeaked in her excitement. "Here…"

"The Parloa plots?" He didn't look up and lose his place like she had.

"Yes! Here is Ba, that must be him only abbreviated. He's to the right of Ella, and she's to the right of John. At least, I'm hoping that's what El and Jhn mean."

"I believe you are correct." He moved around next to her, waiting politely until she had placed her magnifying glass as a marker to the plots and moved away. Then he, with his larger magnifier, leaned in and took a closer look. "Yes, that looks very likely. They aren't graves, you know, this symbol indicates a family crypt. Now, where is Benny's mausoleum from there?"

"It's over here, sir." She pointed at an intersection some distance from his finger on the Parloa plot. "And there is where the ghost is."

"Curious, is it not?"

"What?" Chloe looked at the map. She knew the area where the Parloa plot was. It was deep in the worst of the invasive brush that needed to be cleared. But she didn't think there was anything weird about it.

Well, as far as was possible in Belleview to be normal.

"How little a distance from here to there can make one lost." He tapped his short fingernail against the inked letters. "Have you given any thought about how you are to get young Bartholomew to his grave?"

Chloe frowned in thought. "I was just going to..." She couldn't take him by his hand. She wasn't sure if he'd be able to ride on the cart, last night he'd just kind of sunk into it. "Lead him there? Slowly?"

"Sadly, as I am unable to monitor the grounds as I once was, you shall have to be my eyes, ears, hands and feet." He sat down in one of the chairs and stared into space.

Chloe stayed quiet. She recognized deep thought. He was tapping the magnifying glass gently against his knee. She sat down, too, but kept looking at the map, trying to make out more of the paths that were either overgrown, or had been removed entirely in the ensuing century.

"I rather think that is the best plan." He stood up and walked quickly toward the window. The blinds were drawn. They were always drawn, Chloe had noted. He flicked at one quickly, then nodded. "Still light enough. I shall come with you."

She blinked. "Are you sure, sir?"

"Certainly. A little fresh air and sunshine will do me good." He picked up an ivory-headed cane from the stand by the door. "Let us go scout the locale, Miss Brandt."

Chloe followed him outside. Light was a relative term. It was very near sunset, and the sunshine was a heavy gold trimmed with deep green shadows where it slanted across the trees but not through them.

"I'll bring the cart, then?" She asked.

He stood on the steps; his nose lifted high like he was sniffing the air. "Eh? Oh, certainly. That is an excellent idea."

The third evening in a row, Chloe navigated the cart into the green path at twilight. It was almost a tunnel of brush and trees, and darker than the rest of their journey had been. Mr. Cruor sat next to her, bolt upright, with his cane in between his knees. When she had pulled up in front of the house in the cart to pick him up, he regarded it with such a look of alarm and suspicion, Chloe began to wonder just whose idea the cart had been. What had her predecessor been like? Mr. Cruor climbed up into the cart a trifle awkwardly, and positioned himself on the seat before acknowledging that he was ready for them to go.

And now here they were in pursuit of the lost ghosts. She wondered if her days would ever seem normal again. Since starting this job, the weird only seemed to be accelerating. She put the cart in part and turned off the key.

Silence fell around them. There was the screaming of cicadas, and chirping of crickets, but there was no sign of the ghost. Chloe looked sideways at Mr. Cruor. He had his eyes closed and seemed to be completely ignoring her presence.

"This is where..." She broke off because Mr. Cruor had raised one slim, pale hand to silence her.

Chloe closed her lips obediently and looked around. There wasn't much to see at this time of the day. The shadows were deep under the trees now. A little bit of light remained, nothing like the golden light of the sunset time. The light they had driven through as she slowly putted away from the big house towards this far corner of the cemetery. Chloe was left to sit and think in silence. She wondered if maybe the reason Bartholomew didn't come out of hiding was that Mr. Cruor was there with her. Maybe she should have parked further away and walked down here to meet him, before revealing that she had someone else with her.

She became aware of the faint sound of whimpering somewhere off to her left. She turned her head that way to look but didn't see anything. She looked back at Mr. Cruor and saw that although his eyes were still closed his head was inclined slightly in that direction. She looked back again and startled, her whole body twitching. Bartholomew was standing right there looking at her.

"You scared me." Chloe scolded him.

He hung his head, "I didn't mean to."

"It's all right. I came with good news." She offered, and his head popped back up. He was as clear as she had seen him. The expression on his face was easy to read. A look of eagerness spread over it, and he asked, "you found it?"

Chloe nodded. "We did. I know right where it is and I can take you there."

Bartholomew looked at the cart with a dubious expression. "I don't think..."

Mr. Cruor spoke for the first time since Bartholomew had appeared. Bartholomew's eyes flew to Chloe's boss and got very big.

"No, we will walk with you to your grave."

The walk to Bartholomew's grave was a strange procession. By unspoken agreement, Mr. Cruor took the lead, leaning on his cane as he walked slowly and silently. Bartholomew hung back, almost reluctant, but Chloe urged him on. "We are hoping that the grave will help you rest." She explained to him. "Come on, it's not far."

He walked beside her, and they caught up with her boss quickly. Chloe modulated her steps, and realized that Bartholomew was moving his legs, but it wasn't quite walking. And he tended to just move through objects in his way rather than around them.

The moon rose, and in the silvery light it cast down on them, the ghost looked more solid than ever.

"Look." Chloe pointed. "That's it, I think."

His family was all laid to rest in one of the mausoleums that dotted the landscape around them. Low, Chloe suspected partly underground, it boasted two simple Grecian columns at the front which faced down the steep hillside. The peaked roof projected back into the ground level with the earth behind it. In context, it made some sense, as the slope here was difficult to walk on. Or mow, as Chloe was familiar with this section and maintained it.

Bartholomew turned to her, and the moonlight caught on twin sparkles on his cheeks.

"Are you crying?" Chloe asked without stopping to think about how boys felt about emotional revelations.

"I'm afraid." He said, and his lip quivered as he spoke.

Mr. Cruor walked up to the mausoleum door, and

stopped a little. He was too tall to stand under the tiny portico the columns made.

"It will be fine." Chloe assured the young-looking ghost. "Your family is all here."

"Will you come with me?" The boy asked, holding out his hand as he stood on the marble slab just outside the heavy wrought-iron door. It was chained shut, Chloe noted, with a heavy rusted padlock that looked old. She tried to remember when the last burial here had been.

"I can't, not inside." She pointed at the door. "I haven't got the key."

"I can take you." Bartholomew gave her a watery smile. There were sparkles of moonlight trailing down his cheeks. "Please."

She looked down at his hand, which was pale, but firm-looking. She hesitated and glanced at Mr. Cruor, who the ghost was ignoring. Her boss stood very still, but he shook his head, just a little.

"You can do it." She told Bartholomew in what she hoped was an encouraging tone. "I couldn't get in, anyway."

"If you take my hand, I can carry you in with me." He said it again.

"That's not how this works." Chloe walked right up to the wrought iron gate. Behind it was a more pragmatic solid door, she couldn't tell what that was made of in the dark.

"I'll show you." Bartholomew walked up to the gate and melted partway through it. One hand extended toward Chloe. "Come with me. Please."

Behind her, Mr. Cruor coughed, a small noise, but it reminded Chloe that he was there. She shook her head. The hand disappeared.

She looked back at Mr. Cruor. "Do you think it's all right?"

"Would you like to check?" He pulled a huge ring of keys from his pocket.

"Wow. Do you have the key?" Chloe looked at it. "Shall I call him back?"

"No. I don't think so. But you can go in…" He located a key. "I think this may be it."

She took it when he offered it, and started to put it in the padlock, then hesitated. "What's, er, what's in there?"

"Coffins in crypts. You won't see bodies, Miss. Brandt."

Relieved, Chloe wrestled with the old lock. "This isn't cooperating… oh. There. When was it last opened?"

"I honestly don't know. I don't remember ever opening it." He took the keys back from her while she pried the lock fully open.

"I wonder if he's ok." She tugged on the inner door. That one was metal, old, and unlocked. It swung outward a bit, then stuck. Cloe put her weight on it, but it only came out a few more inches. She put her head in. "Bartholomew?"

The inside was indescribably musty. She sneezed and backed out. "I think he's gone."

"Perhaps." Mr. Cruor took her place and shone a little flashlight into the vault. "Oh."

Chloe saw it. She knew from his tone something was wrong, and then the light slid over a pale dome lying on the floor. "There are skulls… whole bodies in there."

"Step away, Chloe." He started to shut the uncooperative door.

"No, I need to see…" She slid inside, carefully not stepping on them. "Light?"

"Miss Brandt!" He sounded upset, but the light came back on. "What are you…"

Chloe crouched. "Look." She pointed, and the light followed her finger. "That's 70s floral fabric."

She moved her hand to point at the other body. "The one underneath, that shoe… that's fifties."

"How do you know these things?"

"I'm into fashion." She shivered, and looked behind her. The small room was empty other than the crevices in the walls, which were covered by small doors.

"He brought them in here, didn't he?" She stood up. "I want out now."

Mr. Cruor stepped quickly out of her way, and Chloe walked several feet out into the moonlight, taking deep breaths.

"Are you quite all right?"

"No." Chloe said. "I'm not. I would have gone with him, if you hadn't been here. I didn't think that through."

"That he would have had to bring you out again?" Mr. Cruor walked up next to her, near, but not touching. She appreciated that. He was leaning on his cane and gazing up at the moon. "I wasn't certain. I had no idea he had done this before. It simply seemed… odd. That he was so fixated on you he forgot I existed."

"But you did, and you saved my life." Chloe shivered again. "Those poor girls, they must…"

"Try not to think about it. You were sensible not to come alone. They would have had no idea, poor things. Can you imagine telling someone you were trying to help a ghost?"

"Besides you?" Chloe looked up at him, his eyes clear and shining in the moon's reflection. "No. I see."

"Perhaps you do. You are a remarkable young woman." He looked down at her. "What do you plan to do next?"

"Call the cops."

He raised an eyebrow, but said nothing.

Chloe sighed. "It will be a frightful disruption, I know, but those girls... they have family somewhere." She suddenly felt a deep bubble welling up in her chest. "I'm going... gonna cry."

The sob wrenched out of her against her will. "I could be in there with them." She managed in a strangled gasp.

"You are not." A gentle hand rested on her shoulder. "Have you a mother?"

Chloe nodded. Her throat had closed up and she couldn't speak.

"Shall I call her?" He asked.

Chloe shook her head frantically. "She... worries."

"Would you like me to notify the police?" His hand was still resting on her shoulder, and she was trying to stop shaking.

"N - no. In the morning." She sucked in a breath and forced herself to hold it, to stop the convulsive sobs. "I'll call and say that the bodies were found during routine maintenance. Can't say I was lured in by a ghost."

"No, that won't do." He dropped his hand from her shoulder as she regained control of herself. "Routine maintenance would have caught this long ago. I rather think that you will find in the morning that the lock is broken and someone attempted burglary. When you entered, you found the bodies and called."

Chloe straightened her shoulders. "Ok. One more night won't hurt them." She didn't ask who was going to break the lock. She didn't want to know.

"Good girl. Now. Shall we get cocoa before you retire for the night?"

"I'm not sure I want to sleep." She admitted as they walked back toward the cart. She noticed he was moving faster now, even in the dark. He'd been moving like an old man for Bartholomew's benefit, she realized. "I'll have nightmares."

"If Benny hasn't given you nightmares yet, I imagine you will be fine shortly. Your routine will give you solace." He climbed up on the cart and sat waiting for her to drive.

"Yeah." Chloe wasn't so sure of that.

"It's peculiar, how we can come to a place and realize that it is right for us, in spite of conventions."

She wasn't sure that was directed at her. It sounded like he was talking about himself, as he looked around at the moonlit gravestones. She had to admit that in the dark, the cemetery was an eerie but beautiful sight.

"I took the job as caretaker and groundskeeper." Chloe began. "I just didn't realize how far 'care' went."

He looked over at her. "You take care of all herein? Also," He offered her a ghost of a smile, "You attempt to keep in the ground what should be in the ground."

"It's my job?" Chloe wasn't sure what he meant.

"And you are, above all, dutiful and honorable."

They pulled up in front of the big house. Warm golden light spilled from some of the windows.

"I just do my job. Even when it's weird, it's still my job."

"I see. I think you will do well here." He climbed out. "But now, cocoa!"

That sounded good to Chloe. She turned off the cart and followed him into the warmth. There was one last chill brush of wind at her cheek, and then she closed the door on the night.

CHAPTER 2
THE HOODOO YOU DO

"Did you get your ghost laid to rest?" Mark greeted Chloe as soon as she entered the library archive room. Deep in the basement under the city's public library, the vast room full of microfiche files was off limits to the general public. Chloe, to her consternation, had discovered on her first visit to the library for research, the room was not considered general, or public, but was freely open to her because of her place of employment. Or possibly some consideration for her boss. She still wasn't clear on that.

Working as a groundskeeper and caretaker for a cemetery was supposed to be about mowing grass and trimming bushes. Perhaps some light carpentry. Stuff she was good at. Within a month of working at Belleview Cemetery, she'd discovered that taking care of ghouls, ghosts, and various other undead was all considered part of the job. Along with perks like having full access to private areas of the Public Library, it seemed. Which was useful, as this job was turning out to be more of an education than college would have been.

Also...

"*My* ghost?" She put her hands on her hips.

The ghost standing in front of her had the grace to look slightly ashamed of himself. "Well, you *were* looking for him."

"I was looking for his grave. I found it. He tried to kill me, like he'd done with two other girls before me."

Mark Long, associate professor of Oriental Studies, who had been dead longer than Chloe had been alive, wavered slightly more transparent, then nearly corporeal. She almost couldn't see through him.

"What?" His voice came out between a squawk and a wheeze. "What... how... why...?"

She made a face. "It's a long story."

"Will you tell me?" Mark waved his hand toward one of the long reading tables with their antique chairs. Padded and covered in leather, Chloe thought they were probably comfortable. At least, the two library cats seemed to enjoy curling up on their seats.

"Why do you think I came back?" She headed for the chair Esmerelda was snoozing on. Kung, the monster black tomcat, was far less approachable. He cracked one golden eye to see who was disturbing them, then closed it again. The ragdoll, though, opened her brilliant blue eyes, then yawned, showing off all her dainty white fangs against pink mouth. She consented to being resettled in Chloe's lap.

"Really?" Mark sat across the table from Chloe. She still didn't know how he did that. All the ghosts she'd met so far hadn't been able to interact with physical objects. Although... She shivered at the thought of one who had promised to hold her hand. And what would have happened if she had taken him up on that adventure.

"I thought it would be mean never to come back again,

when you were so helpful." Chloe explained. She didn't tell him that she could use more help. She was still trying to figure out the questions to ask. And asking a human seemed like a very bad idea. One that could get her locked up and medicated out of her mind. "So, yeah, I came as soon as I could."

"*As soon...* no." He held up a hand. "I'm sorry, I'm being rude. Are you all right?"

"Yes." Chloe said, then hesitated. She was so used to putting on a stoic front for everyone. Especially for her mother. Even in front of her boss, who had saved her life. "No."

"Were you hurt?" He sounded alarmed.

"Just... scared. Mostly after. Just at the time, I didn't fully process it." Chloe put her elbows on the polished wood of the table and propped her head on her hands, staring at the warm honey color of the wood grain. "After, when there were police, and I was busy... I was ok. The nightmares were later."

"What happened?" Mark sounded worried, now, a downgrade from the fear. He understood the hurt wasn't fatal or physical.

"I keep telling myself I'm ok." She propped her head up and looked at him. "I wasn't hurt like those girls he'd taken in there to die with him. And finding their bodies wasn't really scary. It was interesting, like, I could tell what time they'd lived in from their shoes and clothes. It was kind of cool in a weird way."

"And you feel bad about that." He wasn't asking, he seemed to understand.

"Yeah, kinda. But later, I kept dreaming about being locked in with no way out and no air." She shivered again, and cuddled a compliant Esmerelda to her chest. The cat started to purr. "And now, well, I'm not so good with small spaces any more."

"I see."

She narrowed her eyes at him.

"I don't see," he admitted. "But I think I understand a little. Perhaps if you began at the beginning? Or at least when you were leaving here last?"

"Ugh. I don't even know..." Chloe nuzzled Esmerelda's head and then put the cat back on her lap. "Well. I went back and told my boss everything..."

Some time later, and a drink of her waterbottle she'd pulled from her backpack when her throat got scratchy, Mark was up to speed with Chloe's encounter with the murderous ghost she'd been trying to lay to rest.

His jaw had literally dropped open at the end, which made Chloe giggle inappropriately.

"Have you seen him since? What did you tell the police? Wait, did they even come?" He demanded.

"No," Chloe hugged herself, and Esmerelda jumped off her lap. "He's gone for at least a while. Benny..." She stopped and looked up. "Did I explain Benny?"

"The ghoul?"

"Yeah. He said he hadn't seen him before, and has been keeping an eye out since... since that night. I think Mr. Cruor had a word with him. Benny is being weird."

"Well, he is a ghoul." Mark pointed out. "What about the police, then?"

"We called in the morning. They sent one guy, who got a little freaked out when he saw the bodies and Mr. Cruor explained that yes, bodies are supposed to be in cemeteries, but no, these ones did not belong *there*." Chloe rolled her eyes. "The investigation is still going on. TV makes it look fast, but it's not."

"Thank you for coming to tell me all of this." Mark paused. "I... get lonely."

"Same." Chloe's eyes got big and she clapped one hand over her mouth. Her voice was muffled by it when she said, "I don't know why I said that."

"It was true?"

"Yeah," she moved her hands back to Esmerelda's soft fur. "I just try not to tell anyone."

"I'm not anyone." Mark grinned, and shifted so he was almost translucent. "Who am I going to tell?"

"Point." Chloe sat up very straight. "I have a question for you."

Mark may have seen right through her transparent attempt to change the subject, but he obligingly thickened to visible and straightened up himself. "Go on?"

"I'd like to know what... what all I could be dealing with at Belleview." She grimaced. "When I took on the caretaker and groundskeeper job, I had no idea what I was getting into. What 'care' was going to mean. And, well, I've been rolling with it. But I'm starting to feel a little punchy and I don't know what's going to step out of a shadow next and..." She ran out of steam. "I need to know more about what goes bump in the night. I really enjoyed mythology in school, one of the only subjects I did like, actually. There's a reason I'm working at this job."

"And your boss saw something in you. Regular people would have run screaming."

"I don't want to know anything about Mr. Cruor." She shook her head hard. "Not a thing. He's been really nice, and I don't want to know."

Mark blinked. "Um. I don't know anything? So I couldn't tell you?"

Chloe felt herself get hot in the cheeks. "I just need to

know what to expect, in the cemetery. And you know about these things."

"Because I'm a ghost?" He grinned.

"No, because you were a professor and I barely passed high school." She growled at him when she'd finished speaking. "And you're a brat."

He cocked his head. "I'm older than you. Even if I weren't dead, I'd be older. Brat?"

"Unruly child." She stuck her tongue out, and he started to laugh.

Chloe scooped up Esmerelda and buried her face in the cat's long soft fur. She hated baring her soul like this, but she needed answers.

"Hey, I don't mind." Mark's voice was soft. "I'll try to help, that's what friends are for. Forewarned is forearmed, yes?"

Chloe looked up and met his eyes. "Right. *So*. What am I likely to find under my care?"

Several hours later, Chloe stepped out of the last bus, and walked up the sidewalk alongside the high wall of Belleview. She stopped and looked up at it, painted in the warm orange of the setting sun behind her. She thought that she should be dreading coming back here. Especially in light of the conversation she'd been having with Mark, discussing quite seriously the kinds of monsters she might encounter. It wasn't frightful, though. She was relieved to see the ornate iron gates, and although they were closed, she knew that the little side door would be open for her key, and then... she hurried on towards it. The street was more dangerous than anything inside the cemetery.

Her heart was racing when she closed the old oak door with its hammered iron straps, painted black by her own hands after she'd painstakingly cleaned them of the rust they'd developed. Once she'd turned the big key, and then pushed that back into her pocket, she relaxed. She was home.

Her own apartment was over the big stables, which had once held black horses and hearses. It still had a pair of hearses, one shiny steel, the other covered in dust and cobwebs and there were no horses left to pull it anyway. Which Chloe rather regretted. She'd have loved to have a pair of horses to tend. Not that the sprawling cemetery wasn't more than she had time to do, anyway. But horses! She sighed, and instead of heading for her stairs to the studio apartment, she made her way to the big house where she'd find her boss. She had suspicions her boss wasn't - *fully* - human, but she'd learned he was more trustworthy than most people, so she didn't care.

Chloe let herself into the small door at the side of the house, rather than going to the grand double doors at the front. The front was where funerals had once been held, and now it was never opened. She wondered, as she looked around the spacious office and library, when the last funeral had been held at Belleview. Mr. Cruor was not in the office. Chloe wandered over to take a closer look at her favorite painting. It hung on the wall between two big bookshelves, with a pair of armchairs arranged under it to allow people to sit in them and talk to one another. The painting was a sprawling landscape of vivid greens, with trees sweeping out of sight in the midground, and a meadow in the foreground. Behind them… she let out a little hiccup of air as she stared at the painting.

Mr. Cruor appeared beside her, soundlessly.

"The birds moved." Chloe informed him. She felt stupid as soon as the words were out of her mouth. Of course he could see that. And he probably knew…

"The painting does change." He had his hands clasped behind him, and was leaning forward slightly to study it with her. "It reflects the seasons, you know."

"I... didn't. It's fall?" She fumbled for the right way to respond to him.

"Where it was painted, it is spring." He turned to face her then. "The Snowy Mountains, in Australia, Miss Brandt. Shall I have Miss Dear bring tea?"

Chloe realized he was hinting that she should stay. And a flash of intuition told her that he might be as lonely as she was, despite his advanced age and general...inhumanness.

"Yes, that would be nice." She answered him. A bare hint of a smile touched his thin lips, and he turned away, walking toward the hall door. Chloe watched him, thinking that he didn't move like an old man, in spite of his thin silver hair and gaunt, lined face. His back was straight and while he moved with slow dignity, she thought that was more the way he was than any need to be poky.

Chloe headed for her usual spot at the table in the middle of the room. Unlike her last visit, where it had been heaped with books, it was bare and polished, the gleaming wood smelling of lemon oil and beeswax. Miss Della Dear, the Victorian era skeleton turned housekeeper, maintained the big house spotlessly. Chloe had a small qualm when she thought of the mess her own apartment was in. Sitting, she looked around the room, which could have stepped out of the pages of a magazine, if the magazine had been something about English houses. Chloe had the vaguest idea of the style, but this didn't feel like anything American to her. At least not like her home or any other she'd been in growing up.

Behind her, the door opened and closed. Chloe was bending to pull something out of her bag so she didn't look to see. She'd been introduced to the keepers of the house, once, but hadn't seen them before or since. Mr Cruor paused beside her as she put the book on the table.

"Mythologies and Cryptids?" He read the title aloud. She looked up, and saw that his eyebrows were elevated.

"I asked Mark for help on learning more about local spooks. This was written by a local author, so I checked it out, too."

"You could have asked me." Her boss sat at the end of the table and steepled his hands together, looking at her over his narrow fingertips. "But I am pleased at your initiative and willingness to do your own research."

"I... I know I could have asked for help from you." Chloe shrugged. "I've always preferred to do things myself, even if that's asking an expert. Not that you aren't," She hastened to add, "my mom always told me to use more than one source."

"A wise woman." He looked around. "Ah, the tea."

Della pushed the tea cart up next to the table, nodded at Chloe, who nodded back, unsure what the proper etiquette was in dealing with a skeletal woman who was nominally a servant but seemed to boss Mr. Cruor around, at least to hear him talk about it. Then she whisked away, her long skirts moving over the floor with so little motion she might have been floating. Once the door closed behind her, Chloe turned her attention back to the subject at hand.

"I just want to have an idea of, of what might happen." She fumbled for the words to express herself. "It's not like there's a job description, with duties all in black and white, you know?"

"I do realize that you've rather gone deeply into that little clause that says 'other chores and duties as needed.'

One lump, or three?" He smiled at her, holding the little tongs over the bowl full of sugar cubes.

"Three..." He really did know her well, considering how short a time she had been in his employ. "I don't mind." She wasn't talking about sugar now. "I just don't like surprises like this, much."

"I can't say that anyone rational does. And you, my caretaker, are more rational than most people, even those more than twice your age."

Chloe squirmed in her seat at the compliment. He placed the cup and saucer in front of her. "Della has adopted you into the family, I see. We are honored with the Limoges set."

"It's very pretty." Chloe looked at the delicate floral designs on the service. "It's funny how she's much more girly than I am." She looked at the hand she was about to pick up the cup with. Her snake-ringed fingers with their deep violet nails contrasted oddly with the fragile china. "I mean..."

"You are a goth." Mr. Cruor's smile over the rim of his cup was slightly crooked. "That is what they call it these days, yes? Have you seen the work of the excellent Charles Addams? I believe I have a book of his here if you have not."

"I'm a pastel Goth." Chloe sipped her tea. Della had the knack of making it hot enough to get the flavor out of the leaves, but not so hot it burned. "I like lavendars and greys. But yes, also snakes and skulls."

"No spiders?"

She looked up and caught the twinkle. He was teasing her now. "You should just be happy I'm not a glitter Goth!" She shot back at him, deadpan.

Mr Crour shuddered visibly. "I do have my limits of strange."

Chloe giggled and had to set her teacup down until she could stop. She wasn't going to spill the tea on Della's lovely table.

The doorbell rang, and Chloe jumped. Her cup, safely on the table, didn't budge. Mr. Cruor, who had started to lift his for a sip, froze. Only for an instant before the cup smoothly journeyed back to its saucer.

"How... unexpected." He murmured. "I suppose I shall go answer it."

Chloe blinked, then thought of the reaction a normal human would have to meeting Della, or worse, Trunk at the door. Trunk had the personality of a shy scholar, and the face ripped from a rock wall, complete with ferns and mosses. She occasionally helped him mist the hard-to-reach spots and he was very proud of his greenery, explaining to her the rarer specimens and how he had acquired them. Bridge trolls were not your everyday encounter.

"I'll go." She got up.

"I rather think we both ought to go." He was already standing.

"The main gates were closed." Chloe followed him, his long legs making a pace she almost had to trot to match, "I don't know how someone could have gotten in without a key."

"There are ways." Mr. Crour didn't elaborate, and they were in the lobby. The lights were on, and Chloe glanced around her. Whoever had turned on the lights was not in sight.

"Ready?" Her boss, one long hand on the elegantly curved bronze door handle, looked at her. There was a knocking - more like a pounding - on the outside.

Chloe nodded, knowing her eyes were round.

The door swung inwards, and the man on the outside, one hand raised to strike again, stumbled forward in surprise.

"You rang?" Mr. Cruor drew himself up to his full height and looked down his knife-blade thin nose at the stocky policeman.

"I didn't think anyone was going to answer." The policeman, who was in full dark-blue uniform with the bulk of a bulletproof vest under his blouse, straightened up and frowned irritably at the keeper of the cemetery. "You Cruor?"

Chloe didn't think her boss could get any more icy and hoity-toity, but he managed. "I have that pleasure."

"I have something for you. Sergeant said it was to come to you." For the first time, the policeman noticed Chloe. He frowned harder. "I'll need you to sign for it, it's evidence."

Mr. Cruor lost some of the tension he'd been holding himself upright with. "Ah. I see. Very well, then. Come, Miss Brandt."

Chloe trailed after him and down the shallow stairs towards the drive. It was still light enough she could see the motorcycle. The policeman walked to the back of it, and opened one of the rigid saddlebags, pulling out a square box. "You'll sign on the seal."

He offered a pen, and Mr. Cruor meekly signed where indicated, then handed the box off to Chloe, who took it gingerly. It was not heavy, and she resisted the urge to shake it and see if it rattled. Mr. Cruor signed again, this time on a clipboard he was offered. The patrol officer dropped that back into the saddlebag and picked up his helmet. "Sergeant said you were to call him with any questions." He looked at Chloe. "I don't know anything, and I don't *want* to know anything." He crammed on his helmet and swung his leg over the big motorcycle, firing up the engine in almost the same movement.

As he roared away, Mr. Cruor watched him go. His eyes were sunken and shadowed with the dying light. He turned to Chloe when he could be heard again. "There are a few keys to the front gate not in my keeping."

He didn't elaborate, but turned the rest of the way and went back up the stairs they had just come down. Chloe hurried after him, holding the box with both hands. Something shifted inside, something hard. She followed him all the way back to the library. He gestured at the table. "Place the box there."

"What is it?" Chloe asked, feeling more comfortable in this sanctuary.

"An unpleasant surprise, no doubt." He went to his desk and opened a drawer. "Ah. Would you please ring the bell for Miss Della?"

"Sure." Chloe headed for the archaic velvet rope that dangled next to the door and gave it a gentle tug. She knew that this would, in theory, set off a bell somewhere. She'd seen it in a movie. She'd never been out of her allowed part of the house, though. Not that she was forbidden, it was just that the library was permitted, in some unspoken pact.

"She will take the tea service." Mr. Cruor had a roll of something like paper in his hand. "And then we will open the box with proper precaution."

Chloe decided that it would be nice if she cleared the tea things onto the trolley, and had just finished this little chore when Della entered the room. Chloe backed away a little guiltily, but the skeleton just nodded slightly and pushed the trolley out of the room again.

"Now." Mr. Cruor unrolled what he'd been holding,

which turned out to be a heavy paper with plastic lining one side of it.

Chloe looked at it. "That looks like…"

"It is." He cut her off. "If you would place the box on the paper, please, I would like to keep from potentially damaging the table."

Chloe did as she was told, and her boss produced a slender silver blade seemingly from thin air. At her expression, he stopped and let out a rare dry chuckle. "It is not magic, Miss Brandt. Merely a sleeve holster with a clever spring mechanism. I shall show it to you another time, I think you will be intrigued."

Chloe nodded and stepped to his side as he slit the seal and paper tape under it.

"And now…" He murmured, lifting the lid free of the box.

The familiar pale dome of a skull gleamed from the dark interior. They both leaned over the table, staring down at it.

"Um," Chloe broke the long silence. "Is it one of ours?"

"I don't believe so. He said it was evidence."

"Is there a note or something?" Chloe craned her neck to see around the dry bones. The jaw was tucked to the side of the skull, teeth intact. Something about it was odd.

"One moment." Mr Cruor had stepped away, but now he was beside her again. He reached into the box, white cotton gloves on his hands, and gently lifted the skull out.

As it came out of the box, Chloe realized it had been vandalized. There was something in the eyesockets, whitish and oddly rippling…

"Candle wax." She blurted.

"I believe you are correct. And the teeth have been covered in…" He peered closely at them "Gold leaf, very thin, probably crafter's quality."

"The lower jaw is like that, too," Chloe pointed out.

"Mm. Perhaps it was on display, intact." He brought the skull close to his face and inhaled.

Chloe blinked in surprise at him.

"Smell this, Miss Brandt," he offered it to her, cradling it between her hands.

Feeling like she'd stepped even further into the surreal, Chloe took a deep breath.

"That's not.. It's spices. Like food."

"Indeed. No decay here. I wonder..." He rotated the skull until he had the crown in his palm, and peered at the void where a spinal column had once joined the brain.

Chloe shivered.

"Why would the police send you evidence? Was this... did someone kill this skull, er, person?"

"I see no overt signs of trauma. Although the encrustation of wax hides much of the bony structure." He turned the skull so it was facing her and pointed. "You see the way the maxilla bone protrudes? And here, the shape of the nasal opening is quite broad. The eye sockets are occluded, but this corner, here, implies a rectangular rather than rounded aperture. Now, this is indicative of the ethnicity of the person, and the indication along with the spices, lead me to believe that it was a male of African descent who somehow got tangled up with hoodoo."

"I had no idea you could do that." Chloe looked at him with renewed respect. "I mean, I guess you know about bones, living here."

"I was an anthropologist." He set the skull down on the paper carefully. "I studied humans, in all their strangely predictable forms, until I came to the end of a career. It seemed fitting to end at the end, so to speak, so I came here."

"And the police send you puzzles." Chloe commented as he lifted the jaw out of the box with equal care.

"So it seems." He murmured absently, turning the bone over in his hands. "Very interesting. This does not belong to that."

"But the teeth are the same."

"Only in the gold leaf. Look." He set the jawbone on the paper, then lifted the skull onto it. It fit, but it was easy to see that there wasn't a proper match. The jaw was much smaller than the skull and came nowhere near the sockets where it should hinge. Instead it made the expression of the skull look rather silly.

"Why would they do that?" Chloe crouched down to look at it level with the table top. The eyes full of wax and gleaming teeth made it look inhuman.

"Likely found one without the other. You can buy bones online."

She looked up at him, and he nodded. "It's illegal, but still, it is possible."

"So this was... dug out of a grave?"

He shrugged and she stood up again. "I suspect that is why it came to our attention."

"Would we be able to know if it was ours, er, came from Belleview?" Chloe was thinking of the ghost she'd helped get home to his grave.

"Would you notice if a grave had been disturbed?" He returned the skull to the box.

"Yes, of course. Might take me a few days, if they were digging at one end of my circuit." She'd developed a routine, starting on one section and working continuously around a winding route through the big cemetery, to do the routine mowing and maintenance. Special tasks like slowly clearing brush from overgrown patches were much more irregular. "Or," She admitted as she thought more about it, "if they were smart enough to go to the abandoned places."

"Perhaps a patrol in the morning is in order." He turned the jawbone over in his hand, frowning, and then lifted it to smell. "Ah. Not only is this smaller, but it is not an old bone."

Chloe decided she did not want to smell *that,* and he didn't offer it to her.

"That's not ours, then."

"No. The last interment at Belleview was before you were born, and this is not even a month old."

Chloe gulped. "That's not good at all."

"Simply being fresh does not imply that it is from a victim of foul play." He tucked the bone back into the box, and closed the box. "This can wait until morning."

On cue, Chloe yawned. She grimaced as her jaw popped.

"We need to discuss making you salaried." Her boss narrowed his eyes at her. "And taking days *off*. I do mean off, not research trips."

Chloe shrugged. "I wanted to learn more..."

"Which you will do. On paid time. Off paid time, find a hobby. Go see your family. Remember there is a wide normal world out there. And now, get some rest."

He didn't exactly shoo her out the door, but Chloe found herself walking across the wide courtyard to her stairs. The entrance to the apartment over the old stables was on the end, sandwiched at an angle between the big house and the stables. Lit brightly by an LED bulb she'd installed, she walked up the steps, hearing a creak from one and making a mental note to see about tightening it as she pulled her keys from her pocket. Locking the door made her feel less nervous, even if she had learned that some things in the cemetery respected no physical boundaries.

Her apartment was cluttered and smelled of takeout meals past, which her stomach flipped over. It also reminded her that she hadn't eaten since lunch. The little cookies with tea shouldn't count. Her mother was firm about what was, and wasn't, real food. Protein was required at least once a day, but better twice. Chloe dropped her bag on the small couch before heading for the refrigerator. Like the rest of the furnishings in the apartment, it had been there when she got there. Her mother had helped her move in, and had offered to help her find things to make it more her own, but Chloe had declined. She knew her mom loved to scrounge and arrange, and it would have been more cozy, but she'd wanted to do it on her own.

Somehow, that time just hadn't materialized. She stared into the glowing light spilling from the fridge and contemplated that Mr. Cruor was right, much as she dreaded the thought of planning to do something away from the cemetery. It felt aimless, to do something just to not be at home. She did have a hobby. She played video games. She closed the door on the light. There wasn't anything in there that looked edible.

One cup of noodles later, she curled up on the good end of the couch, her feet lightly resting on the part where the springs were gone. Sit there, and you wouldn't get up again easily. She'd hooked up her console to the ancient TV, then had bought a monitor with her first paycheck, giving up on the old tubed monstrosity in it's wood case. The doors had long gone from it, and it weighed about 500 pounds, so it still sat under the slim monitor, the screen a reflective gray. She'd gotten so used to it she never even noticed it anymore.

When it started to glow, she flinched as though it were a physical attack. There was a brief burst of static, then vertical stripes of black and white, then colored bars, and then...

"Della?" Chloe blurted, swinging her legs around to sit up straight. "Is that you?"

The skelton looked primly out of the screen and folded her hands at her waist. "Miss Brandt, I apologize for the intrusion."

"Uh. I didn't know you could do this. Can you see me?" Chloe looked around at her mess.

"I can. I am not judging your personal choices."

Which meant she totally was, but was too polite to say anything, Chloe decided.

"I must ask you to come get that... that thing... out of the house." Della actually sounded upset, the most emotion Chloe had ever seen her display. "Now, I'm afraid I must insist."

"What thing?" Chloe asked cautiously, shoving her feet back into her boots and starting to lace them up. She never knew when she'd need safety toes in this job.

"The package that arrived tonight."

"The skull?"

Della turned her head as though she were looking around wherever she was transmitting from. "Shh! Yes. I cannot have it in the house for a moment longer!"

She was really upset, Chloe could see.

"I'll be right there. Does Mr. Cruor know..."

Della interrupted her. "He does not understand, and has gone up to his room."

"Ok. It's in the library?"

"Yes. I will open the side door for you."

"I'll be right there..." Chloe's voice slid to a stop, as she was talking to a dark screen.

Della's worry had been contagious. She found she was looking around as she crossed the dark yard towards the other side of the house. Nothing moved that she could see, but there wasn't a moon on that night. She was even worrying about finding the steps to the door in the dark, when that door opened and a faint light spilled out and down the stone stair.

Chloe walked up the steps to find Della standing in the doorway.

"It is there." The skeleton pointed, her hand shaking enough that Chloe could faintly hear the dry bones rattle as she walked past her toward the box on the table. "Remove it, please!"

Chloe scooped up the light cardboard cube and walked back toward the door, but Della had somehow moved almost all the way across the room in the short time it had taken Chloe to go halfway.

"I have to bring it back in the morning." Chloe called after her.

"It must never cross the threshold! It should not have come here." Della closed the inner door behind her without a sound, which was somehow more unnerving than a slam would have been.

Chloe sighed, wondered what had gotten into Della, and closed the outside door behind her after making sure it was locked. The trip back to her apartment was equally uneventful. Once up there, she placed the box atop the console, tucked out of sight behind her monitor, which was playing a random video, having moved on from the one she'd been watching before the interruption.

Mr. Cruor would have said if there was something

weird with the skull, other than the jaw being fresh, Chloe reassured herself, and yawned widely. Time for bed. Skull wasn't going anywhere. Della could explain to their boss. Was Della an employee? Given she was dead, Chloe wasn't sure how *that* worked.

Burrowed into the big bed, which she'd half-filled with stuffed animals in defiance of her nominal adult status, Chloe slept dreamlessly. Her alarm woke her, and she reached for it to slap it off, then remembered the skull.

"Darnit." She sat up, spilling a couple of fuzzy things on the floor. "I need to tell him where it went."

Coffee, first. He could call her from the intercom if he really wanted to. She'd been bewildered by the two phones when she first arrived, until he explained that one was a line only between cemetery numbers. It lit up when someone called, and she'd taken to referring to it as the batphone. She was pouring coffee into a travel mug she could carry over to the big house when it started to flash at her.

"Good morning, sir."

"Chloe, did you take the skull?"

"Yes. Miss Dear called me and made me take it."

"Ah." He let out a breath of air she could hear clearly through the receiver. "Was there... any trouble?"

"Slept like a log. Shall I bring it over now?" She looked at the mug on the table, steaming gently.

"No, I think I need to speak with Miss Dear if you don't mind keeping it there for now."

"I can do that. I need to go mow..."

He interrupted her. "That may have to wait, I'm afraid." He used some of the same phrases as Della, and Chloe found herself wondering who picked it up first. "I'll come there when I can."

Chloe looked around nervously. "Yes, sir." She was going to have to do some fast cleaning.

By the time he knocked politely at her door nearly two hours later, the living area of the apartment was quite passably clean, and Chloe was confident he wouldn't be going into her bedroom where rather a lot of clutter was hiding. She would have to tackle that before she'd be able to sleep on her bed again, and sleeping on the couch was simply impossible.

"Hello," She opened the door. "I can put the kettle on?"

He blinked at her in surprise. With a slow smile, he answered, "I would like that. This may take some time."

"All right, then." She stepped back and then closed the door when he walked in.

Her boss was looking around with apparent curiosity.

"You haven't done anything with it?" He asked. "Other than an upgrade to the television I see."

"Well, I haven't really needed anything..." Chloe realized at that moment a glaring deficiency. "Don't sit in that chair. I don't think it will hold up."

He let go of the back of the wooden chair and looked down at it with raised eyebrow.

"It's a bit broken, not that you're heavy or anything." She pushed the other one towards him. "Here."

She rolled her task chair over from it's station by her desk in the corner.

"The skull is behind," She gestured at the big monitor.

"I see." He murmured, but took his seat and watched her prepare their tea things as her electric kettle glowed on the counter. She didn't have limoges, sturdy mugs with animated characters on them would suffice. Hers had a little lid with a cow on it, and Mr. Cruor smiled at it, the lines around his eyes crinkling up.

"How cheerful." He commented, holding up his own mug, which had a line of conga-dancing rabbits cavorting around it.

"I, er, buy cute things that make me happy." Chloe shrugged. She brought the kettle to the table. "I have teas in the box."

The square box in the center of the table was opened and inspected. She had an assortment of teas in there, all different flavors and brands, which she'd collected since she moved out and a lot her mother had sent with her.

"This is wise." Mr. Cruor gravely selected a Lady Grey and tore open the sachet. Chloe wasn't sure if he meant the happy things, or the teas. "I am going to tell you why Miss Dear called you."

"I'm curious about that, yes." Chloe prepared her own tea, waiting for him to start.

"You must understand that she is a product of her own time." He took the honey bear, inspected it briefly, then used it to add a small amount to his tea. The plastic squeeze lemon got him smiling again. "Tea with you is unexpectedly delightful."

Chloe wasn't sure how to take this. Fortunately he didn't seem to expect a response, or maybe he had gotten used to her awkward silences.

"Della tells me there is a malevolent spirit in the skull. Not," He lifted a hand in a *stop* gesture, "a ghost. She further stated that as a good Christian woman, she could not stay in the same house as a 'creature from the abyss' and that is why she asked you to remove it."

"So she sent me home with a cursed skull because..."

"I suspect she assumes your, er, fashion sense implies that you would not be as worried about such a taint."

He wasn't wrong, although Chloe still felt uncomfortable with the idea of an actual demon in her apartment. She joked about them, and it was edgily expected to flirt with being fully anti-Christian, and yet the reality gave her shivers in a way that not even her first encounter with a ghoul had.

"So what now?" That he'd taken two hours in discussions with Miss Dear, and hadn't fully explained that, implied to Chloe that the skull was on her hands for good.

"I think I will remove it from here, albeit not back to the main house. I shall secure it, and you will, I am sorry to say, be diverted from whatever you had planned to do today."

Chloe wrinkled her nose. "Mowing, since it's a nice day."

"I wish I could wait for a rainy day to send you on this mission, but Della was... most upset. Dealing with the skull will be our top priority until we can return it with the information they wanted us to obtain."

"Look," Chloe protested. "This can't be evidentiary, in any way."

He raised an eyebrow. Chloe felt her face get warm. "Mom is... mom talks about her job at home, and I used to listen to lectures."

"Fascinating." He set down the cat mug. "I'm going to send you to do some research. Can you trust your library ghost?"

"Mark? I think so? I think he's lonely and evidently most humans ignore him." She picked up both mugs and walked them to the sink for a rinse. "What am I looking for?"

"I've written down as much information as I can deduce from the bones." He produced a folded sheet of paper, then an envelope. "Here is a per diem fund for you, since you will incur travel costs and presumably be away long enough to need a meal, in addition to any printing costs."

Chloe took the paper, leaving the envelope on the table. "The bus is cheap. And I have a pass."

"Miss Brandt." He stood up, stooping slightly so he didn't tower over her. "You are being employed as a professional, and this is a professional protocol. You need not worry over your independence. You provide a highly valuable service, and are being recompensed for such. Do you understand?"

Chloe shook her head. "I mow! I cut brush! I talk to ghosts, it's not hard!"

"Hard doesn't make the value, you realize. You are extraordinarily apt for the position, and I would like to continue this situation as long as you are willing." His voice was gentle. "I realize you do not understand fully, but you are not an average young lady."

Chloe squirmed.

"Please take it." He offered her the envelope. "I rather think the Beverly has a lovely coffee shop, where you might take your afternoon tea time."

Chloe looked at the envelope. "You're paying me to be your researcher."

"Think of it as caring for Miss Dear, if that helps." His lips quirked at the corners. "In expediting the removal of the skull back to the police. And perhaps the bones back to their proper places in another cemetery."

With a sigh, she took the money. "I'll report in as soon as I can, sir."

"Very good, then. And now, I shall take the skull and lock it in the hearse, since the safe in the house is out of the question. Improvise, adapt, and overcome, Miss Brandt."

Chloe found herself entering the library a couple of

hours later, and with a nod at the librarian manning the front desk, she casually went through the door marked 'authorized personnel only' and down the narrow steps to the microfiche room. The paper in her pocket, and her bag over her shoulders, she was prepared to do the research herself if Mark wasn't around.

He walked out of the stacks as she opened the door, a book in his hand. With a look of surprise, then a smile, he greeted her.

"Back again?"

"My boss sent me to research. I'm being *paid* to research!"

Mark's smile widened to a grin. "Dreamy, isn't it?"

"I'm not a researcher!" She shot back at him. "I have a list of words, and I'm supposed to make sense of them in context of an old skull and fresh jawbone?"

"Oh, that does sound like a good puzzle. Let me see." He laid the book down on the table, and came around to where she'd put the paper flat on the table and looked at it. "Want to elaborate on that context?"

"Why is it that whenever I come here, it's storytime?" Chloe saw Esmerelda emerge from the stacks. She held out a hand and waved her fingers at the cat, who promptly sat down and washed a paw ostentatiously.

"Because I live for your stories?" Mark grinned at her.

The absurdity of what he'd just said struck Chloe and she spluttered. "Ok, then..."

Somewhat later, Mark interrupted her mid-sentence. "You spent the night with a demon?!"

"Well, it was in the other room? And I'm not sure demon is the right word. They said spirit."

"Well, that doesn't make it any better." He looked as upset as he sounded. "That was very unsafe."

"I promise not to do it again?" She looked at the paper. "Does this help any, along with cayenne, nutmeg, sulfur and ass... fetiddy?"

"Asfoetida." He corrected absently. "Pure beeswax, and grave dirt. He said hoodoo, not voodoo or voudon?"

"Yes, and his enunciation is much better than mine." Chloe frowned. "I didn't realize there was a difference?"

"Subtle, but yes, there is. That particular herbal blend means a more West African origin, where hoodoo hails from, through the lens of slavery here in the US. I wonder..." He looked over his shoulder at the stacks of newspapers behind him. They were all in boxes but she'd already learned he was very good at finding the information storehoused in them.

"Do do what you do best." Chloe waved her hands. "I'm really just the messenger."

"Oh, I think you're more than that." He walked away, vanishing around the corner.

Esmerelda, having shown that she could not be called, walked up to Chloe with her tail waving like a banner. Chloe picked her up dutifully and snuggled her. Mark seemed to be taking a long time to return, more than was usual. Esmerelda wanted down, so Chloe obliged, and stood to stretch. Sitting for too long hurt. She moved around the table to look at the book Mark had been reading when she came in.

"Professor Fraedy's treatise on comparative mythology." His voice from behind her startled Chloe. She turned around, a hand to her heart.

"Sorry. I did find something on minkisi, though." He waved a sheaf of papers.

"Mink what?" She stumbled over the odd word.

"Min-key-see." He repeated slowly. "Spirit containers.

You said Mr. Cruor thought the skull was old, and African in shape?"

"Yes, and the jaw doesn't match it."

"These are mimeographs." He laid the papers on the table and stepped back so she could inspect them. "Newsletters from decades ago, from an obscure sect of hoodoo practitioners. Hoodoo doesn't usually use human remains, but if the skull belonged to a particularly holy person, sort of like a saint, that may be what it is, a minkisi. Just… a very powerful container befitting a powerful spirit."

"But not a demon." She said firmly. She'd decided it couldn't be.

"Depends on your definition…" He shut up when she glared at him. "Er, right. So what they should be looking for is a desecrated holy place, a shrine that had a relic stolen. The jaw I can't speak to."

Chloe sat with the papers and started making notes from the somewhat smudgy text. "Well, if it's still as fresh as Mr. Cruor thought, I think it can have DNA tests done."

Mark, who watched modern television, nodded. "And the sect whose relic was stolen may be looking for their skull."

She looked up, frowning. "But would they be, um, would they talk to the police?"

"Probably not. Your boss, on the other hand, is tapped into the underworld." He grinned. "In a very literal sense."

"This at least gives us clues to pass on to the police, I guess." She decided not to think about the underworld comment. "Thank you."

"My pleasure. Come again any time." He waved his hand at the stacks. "My home is always open to you."

"I really hope I don't have to come too often."

The look on his face, of crushed feelings, caught Chloe,

and she hastily added. "Not for this kind of reason. Maybe just to hang out?"

He smiled. "I'd like that. Puzzles are fun, but so is conversation. Besides, I'm still working on that city mythos project, because it was something I hadn't come up with on my own, even if I am part of it."

Chloe decided she didn't need to rush back. "Tell me about it. You get too close to something, and you lose perspective. Maybe I can help? Be a sounding board if nothing else. And I need to know." She glanced ruefully at the stack of papers. "Since literally anything can happen at the cemetery, it seems."

"Right, then!" Smiling, he appeared to sit across the table from her, and leaned on his elbows, talking with great animation.

Chloe smiled back and listened to her friend do what he loved best.

CHAPTER 3
MY GHOUL

JUMP SCARE

She yawned with jaw popping force, and Mark flinched. Chloe shook her head and picked up her mug, before realizing it was empty. She reached for her thermos and shook it, then poured some of the contents in the mug.

Mark eyed the dark liquid suspiciously. "What are you drinking?"

"Cold tea." Chloe took a gulp.

"Iced tea?" He cocked his head slightly to one side.

She shrugged. "Iced implies intent. This is just gone cold. But it's wet and contains caffeine and I don't feel like going for an energy drink."

"You'll have to explain that to me, as well." He'd already asked her a hundred questions about the world outside the library.

"Can you not leave..." she waved her hands around. "Here?"

"I..." He stopped, his mouth partly open. He was sitting

across the table from her, the stack of books and papers between them. "I have a confession."

"You're not a ghost." Chloe sounded as irritable as she felt. She was tired, and Mr. Cruor had been firm about the urgency in this task.

"No, I'm a ghost. I'm also feeding off your energy." Mark stood up, and she realized that he was faded almost to invisibility below the waist, where he'd been out of her sight. "I can't take shape without energy, and tapping into electricity is dangerous."

"So you're vamping me?" Chloe knew she should be upset, but all she was feeling at the moment was relief that she hadn't become immune to caffeine.

"Er... Yeah, I guess." Mark lifted his palms. "I've been enjoying our chats."

"And you're helping me. A lot. I'm not a researcher, I'm a caretaker and groundskeeper. Much easier for me to mow, or use a machete on brush. So. Let's go to the coffeeshop." Chloe stood up. "I'm going to need some sugar and chocolate."

"There's a problem with that." Mark didn't bother fully forming, which Chloe guessed was out of consideration for her current state.

"Yeah?" She stopped with one hand on the doorknob. "Can you really not leave the library?"

"I can. I think. I can't go far, though." He waggled his hand. "I haven't really tried, but there's a very strange phenomenon..."

Chloe held up a hand, cutting him off. "You can explain quantum mechanics to me when I've had something in my stomach. Can you go as far as the Beverly?"

The once-grand hotel turned into boutique shops and conference center stood catty-corner to the impressive city library. Which meant it was only a few hundred feet from the basement room where they were standing.

"Yes." Mark didn't elaborate on this certain answer, and Chloe didn't ask.

Normally, she'd avoid the artisanal coffee shop that sprawled across one side of the hotel's lobby. It was a bit more than her budget would allow. Today, though, Mr. Cruor had handed her an envelope with cash. Spend it, he'd ordered. Chloe wondered if she would have argued more had her stomach not growled at him. She'd gotten breakfast, and now she was getting tea, a full, *proper* tea. Fueling both her and Mark was draining. Not that she'd realized she was doing that before, or she would have packed a protein bar.

Juggling a large cup of the spiced, smoky Russian tea she'd discovered recently, along with a white chocolate, orange, and dried cranberry scone, she ignored Mark. So did everyone else, she'd noticed. He was right next to her, head on a swivel, and when she sat, so did he.

"You're facing the door," he commented, continuing to look around with avid interest. "You don't do that in the library."

Chloe hooked her earbuds in ostentatiously, then answered him like she was responding to a conversation through them. "Door's locked. I don't need to."

"Oh." He contemplated her food. "I thought you wanted chocolate?"

"Tea and sugar. Might get a brownie to go." Chloe took a bite. "Mmm."

"I do miss taste," Mark admitted. "And smell."

"Seems like if you're going to use me as a battery, you should be able to sense what I do?" Chloe took a sip of her tea.

Mark shook his head as she looked expectantly at him. "No, I can't read your mind."

"Well, that's a relief."

"Speaking of mind reading, since I assume you don't want to talk about the research out loud in public, why don't you eat while I tell you a story." He folded his hands on the table and she looked through them at the polished wood grain.

"It's a plan." She bit her scone again.

"The ghoul's lair was..."

He broke off and turned around as she reacted to something behind him, with wide eyes and sitting up straight, back stiff.

A man had run into the hotel lobby. He stopped, looking around in complete bewilderment. In one hand he carried a large pair of shears, the blades partly opened. He raised them, and waved them wildly, his mouth opening and closing. No one so much as looked at him, and he didn't seem to notice Mark and Chloe staring from across the room. He turned, and ran back out again. Right through the closed glass doors with their old fashioned brass handles.

"That was a..."

"Ghost," Mark finished for her when her sentence ended in a gasp. "Can you run and eat at the same time? I'd like to catch up with him."

"No." She picked up her drink and crammed her scone into her bag. "Let's go!"

They dashed across the lobby, Chloe weaving between bemused shoppers, and out the doors where the ghost had vanished. Chloe stopped dead on the sidewalk, right on the curb, and looked around. There was nothing besides a scattering of regular everyday people.

"He went this way." Mark's voice got her attention, and

she turned toward him. He had nearly dematerialized, leaving only a mirage shimmer of himself in the air. "I can see... traces that you cannot."

"That's useful." Chloe walked briskly after him. "Why are we chasing this guy, again?"

"I want to know his story. I'm a historian!" Mark sounded indignant, although she couldn't see his expression. They turned into an alley.

"So why am I involved again?" Chloe was wondering what would happen if their quarry had slipped through a wall.

"Same reason I got involved when you showed up at the library. Both times."

"Curiosity? I'd make a crack about what happened to the cat, but you've already done that." She'd learned that Mark didn't think of being dead as a bad thing, and she enjoyed twitting him. "Besides, the first time I was researching a serial killer who'd been killing after death. This time it's just weird."

"Best kind of research project." Mark had stopped at the foot of a set of metal stairs. They led up to a loading dock, and a door, about four feet from the alley surface. "Not today, I guess."

"You can't go in there?" Chloe looked up at it. She didn't see a camera, but she really didn't want a trespassing charge, either.

"You can't. So I won't. Besides, we left your teacher's notes sitting on the table in the microfiche room."

She headed back toward the library door, his wispy self flanking her. "Not really notes. It's weird. I went to the mailbox and there was a package from a teacher I had years ago."

"How long have you been out of school?" Mark was

right beside her even in the narrow subterranean hall that led to the research room that she had been given the key to. She wasn't sure anyone else used it or at least she'd never seen anyone.

"Two years, now. So this was like... four years ago. The weirdest thing is that it showed up at work. Addressed to me. So he knew I was there at Belleview?" She unlocked the door and went into the room. She probably wasn't supposed to have food and drink in here. At least her coffee had a lid. The scone she would just eat over her bag to catch any crumbs. Not that a mouse would dare set foot in here. Not with Esmeralda and Kang on patrol. The cats had come to greet her earlier, then disappeared again to do cat things.

"Probably the news coverage." Mark pointed out, shimmering into partial visibility.

"Oh. Right. *That.*" Chloe was disgusted. "My luck, it was a super slow news cycle."

"People are interested in crimes. Like your teacher."

The package from Mr. Gray had been nothing more than a stack of newspaper clippings. Not even an explanatory note. Chloe had packed them back up after a bewildered few minutes of looking through them, and taken them to her boss. Mr. Cruor had set his teacup carefully to one side, and spread them out over the top of the table in his study, pursing his lips as he read them. He'd turned them over from time to time to see what was on the other side, which mystified Chloe until he'd raised his head and looked at her.

"Some of these are quite old." He pointed at the advertisements on the back of one article. "And some are more recent. I think if you were to arrange them in chronological order, that would be helpful."

"How?" Chloe had looked down at them, her brow furrowed. "There's no dates on any of them."

"Ah! A good question. I think the answer may lie at the library, and I suggest a trip forthwith."

"I have work…"

He raised a single slender white finger. Chloe stopped talking.

"This is work."

She blinked at him, and he gave her a faint smile. "The package came to the cemetery. It deals with the unexplained. Ergo, it is work. I pay your wages, child, and will give you a per diem for the day spent in the city."

Which was when he'd given her the cash. Chloe had boarded the bus, and now, here she was. Albeit a small side track having been taken chasing a random ghost.

"So," she said aloud to Mark. "All of these are about missing women."

Chloe had spread all the clippings out on the long table, and it covered a depressing amount of space. Looking at the paper, she could see what Mr. Cruor had spotted - that some of them were yellowed and brittle, while others were less so.

"Fifty-eight of them." Mark was walking around the table, which was less eerie than walking through it, Chloe had to admit.

"My boss wanted me to make a timeline." Chloe gestured. "By finding the newspaper they had been printed in. I don't even know where to start with that."

"We can start the hard way, or the easy way." He grinned at her.

Chloe narrowed her eyes at him. "The hard way is microfiche…?"

"The easy way is I go looking for them." His smirk

increased, something she hadn't thought possible. Then he burst into laughter. "The look on your face!" he gasped after a minute.

"It occurs to me you could have done this before. And instead, I spent hours..." She put her hands on her hips. "You..."

He waved his hands, palms toward her, still smiling broadly. "Would you have believed me? I mean, you were comfortable with me from the beginning. Oddly accepting. But if I had offered to do it for you?"

She plopped back into a chair and put her elbows on the edge of the table, ruffling but not moving any of the clippings. "Probably not." She put her chin in her hands and stared down at them. "I've always been independent."

"That's easy to see from the first time I laid eyes on you." Mark put a hand on the table, and she eyed the way it was not-quite-touching the surface.

"How do you do that?" she asked abruptly. "I know, I asked before, but this isn't really about your spatial awareness, which most other ghosts..."

"She's known so many..." he murmured, and Chloe ignored his snark.

"You have a sense of reality. Like..."

"Like I'm a real person?" He went very serious, and she flinched from the look on his face.

"Yeah. Sorry."

"Not something to apologize for." He sat so he was eye to eye with her across the table. She decided not to notice there was no chair where he was. "You treat me like I'm real. The librarians don't acknowledge me even if they see me. Researchers who make it down here?" He spread out his hands and made an exaggerated shrug, the shoulders of his suit coat rising and falling. "I'm just happy no idiotic ghost hunters have decided the library basement is a good place to look."

She blinked. "Would they be able to see you?"

"Heh... I don't know." Mark shook his head. "The library breakroom tv is on all the time. But rarely on that channel, and I can't tell if any of it is real. The show."

"That explains your grasp of pop culture." Chloe tapped her finger on the wood, tracing the grain. "Also... the other ghost. Why didn't you follow him?"

"Didn't want to get you in trouble," he replied without a hesitation. "Humans have laws."

"Ghosts don't?" She looked into his eyes. He was solid enough to see expressions in them.

"Not in the same sense. That would require community..." His lips quirked up on one side. "Do you really want me to start in on a history lecture, or sociology perhaps?"

She laughed. "I keep forgetting you were a professor. I think of you as being my age, hiding from work obligations at the library."

"Oh, I did some of that." He got up and headed for the racks of the storage room, with their stacks of boxes full of papers. "Oldest to newest?"

Chloe took a second to switch tracks from talking about ghostly society back to the reality of the papers in front of her. "Seems reasonable."

"On it." He vanished by the simple expedient of walking between the racks and out of sight. Chloe found this reassuring. He really did work at not being spooky for her.

DON'T BE A JERK

Chloe looked down at the clippings while she waited. The downside of this was that she didn't have anything to do while he went looking. After reading a few of the articles she started to feel uneasy. It wasn't the topic. And she didn't think it was how little detail was given in the reports. It was...

She spun around.

Standing behind her was the ghost from the coffee shop. His head hung down almost to his chest, and he faded slowly away until his feet were not visible, giving him the effect of hovering in midair. He slowly extended one hand toward her, the other hand, the one holding the big metal shears, hanging limply by his side.

Chloe gulped around the lump in her throat.

"Wha... what do you want?"

He opened his fist, and there, lying on his palm, was a bloody eyeball.

Chloe heard her own hiss of breath as she inhaled, hard.

The eye blinked at her.

"Mark!" Her shriek was loud enough to make the ghost in front of her bobble backwards, his hand closing around the eye reflexively.

Mark, half materialized, whooshed past her and got into the other ghost's face. "What do you mean by this?" he demanded, reaching out toward the fading figure.

"I'm sorry! I'm sorry!" The other ghost drifted backward, away from Mark, and into the microfiche desks. He raised his now empty hands. "Dude. I just... I was gonna scare her."

"Well, you did. Bravo. Now, why are you trying to be a jerk?" Chloe, her heart still pounding, put her hands on her hips. "Mark, didn't you tell me electricity was dangerous to a ghost?"

Mark crossed his arms over his chest, and leaned back slightly. The other ghost stopped, looking confused.

"Yes, it is. And those machines are old enough to be slightly more powerful than the computers upstairs, which just tingle when you waft through them."

"The fact that you interact with electricity at all is kinda weird," Chloe told him, ignoring the other ghost, who was now looking around frantically but carefully not moving. "Since you can't really interact with me on a physical level. Just on the mental."

"So are you ready to talk now and not be a total ass?" Mark asked of their intruder.

"What are you doing to me?" The other man had a strange accent Chloe couldn't place. His use of modern vernacular meant he was recently dead, she thought. Then again, Mark had haunted the library for almost a century and talked like he was still alive and with it.

"Not doing anything." Mark continued to crowd the ghost.

"And we won't," Chloe interjected, "If you'll talk and not keep trying to scare me. I know you can't hurt me, you just surprised me."

Mark gave her a strange look, which Chloe filed away to ask about later, when she was certain they were alone. Then he refocused on their guest.

"We tried to talk to you earlier, and you ran. What made you seek us out now?"

"She could see me." The ghost shrugged and sidled sideways, away from the machine he'd nearly drifted into. "Look, it's not that common to see one of us. And I've never seen a human notice me at all before."

"Funny. I seem to meet a lot of ghosts." Chloe stopped and thought about it. "I definitely talk to more dead people than living ones."

"You're odd, my friend," Mark told her, his tone solemn but his eyes dancing with laughter.

"Proudly." She turned back to the other ghost. "I'm sorry, I should introduce myself. I'm Chloe, and I'm the groundskeeper at Belleview."

"And I am Dr. Mark Long." Mark made a sketchy bow in the direction of the other, which Chloe noted had a sarcastic overtone to it. She hadn't known you could do that with a bow.

"Er. I am... Satya Jain."

Mark leaned back and uncrossed his arms, resting his palms just slightly above the surface of the long table like he was leaning against it. "Really? Is it now?"

Satya looked away.

"Let him be," Chloe told Mark. "Is it important what his name really is?"

"Yes, since he just said his first name means truth." Mark shook his head. "I'm offended on behalf of jainism."

"No one can pronounce my real name." The ghost claiming the name wavered. "If I am dead, I can claim a new name?"

"Fine by me. So, Satya, why did you track us down? And why did you try to scare me?" Chloe stepped a bit in front of Mark, and locked eyes with the recently dead.

"You scared me." He shifted his eyes away from her, and Chloe suddenly wondered why he didn't just vanish. He didn't have to stick around, it wasn't like she could do anything at all to him. She looked over at Mark. She realized she had no idea what, if anything, ghosts could do to one another.

"Why, because I can see you?" There had been an awkward pause before she spoke, but no-one acknowledged it.

"No human has *ever* seen me before." He locked eyes with her, and she realized he really did look frightened. "I've tried. I tried so *hard*, at... at first."

"You're lonely." Mark was still in his relaxed impossible pose. Chloe wondered if he'd practiced it. She knew he made an effort to not float through things to help her feel he was... human.

"You're a ghost," They both looked at her like she'd grown a second head. "And you don't know what that means, or anything." Chloe shrugged. "Worse than puberty. It's a huge change, and you're having trouble adjusting."

"Life has an end." Mark looked and sounded sad. "This... is limbo."

"Yeah." Satya put his hands up and covered his face. The scissors and eyeball had vanished.

Chloe wondered what the significance of the scissors was.

"There's a way to end it," she offered. He didn't look up. "If you go back to your grave..."

He interrupted her, his voice muffled behind his hands, a trick since they had no real substance. "Haven't got one."

Chloe shrugged and looked at Mark, who sighed soundlessly.

"Ok, then, you can help us." Chloe looked at her watch. "I'm supposed to be back in three hours to tell my boss what I found, and you're taking time I'm being paid to do something else."

Mark blinked. Satya pulled his hands away from his face and looked at her with an incredulous expression. Chloe uncrossed her arms and put her hands on her hips. "You made me scream. You owe me."

"What.. what happens after I help you?" Satya asked.

"Well, the cow fortress has been suspiciously vacant recently. I can put you up there."

"Cow fortress?" Satya and Mark both repeated with a look of mutual confusion.

"I call it that because it's got cows. Bulls, really, and it's built like a fortress. Almost pagan, which is weird in all the Christian imagery. Mr. Cruor has a book I've been reading... What?" She stopped talking when they both stared at her, jaws dropping open.

"Belleview." Mark turned and looked at Satya. "She's talking about the cemetery where she works."

"What did you think I was talking about?" Chloe pulled a chair out. "Although what my boss is going to say about my bringing home strays..." She dropped her voice an octave. "Don't you have enough to do without adopting the undead, Chloe?"

Satya started to laugh, a tinge of hysteria to it. When he could talk again, he gasped. "I will help. You are..."

"She's peculiar," Mark put in with a smirk at Chloe. "Friendly to... well, I'm not going to spoil it. I'm going to get back to work."

"You work for her?" Both of them headed toward the racks of stored papers.

Mark's voice trailed behind him as he plunged into the search and out of sight. "Not really..."

Chloe found herself alone at the table full of papers once more. She looked down at them, then turned away. Life had taken more surreal turns in the last few months than even she could take without it shaking her, in this case literally as she felt a shudder run down the length of her body. Why had her teacher chosen her, of all people, to send these clippings to? Why had he saved them at all? She did the mental math for the first time, and realized that either he was a lot older than he looked, or some of these...

Mark popped back into sight, around the end of a rack. He was always good about being natural with these things, and at the moment she really appreciated the almost-aliveness of it.

"Hey, found one! It's from 1899."

That meant for certain Mr Grey had not been alive when it happened. So, where had he gotten the clipping from? And again, why?

Chloe repeated her thoughts aloud to Mark, who shrugged. "Perhaps he was researching for a project?"

"Like a book?" She frowned at the microfiche reader. She really didn't like them, but the papers were too old to be handled when you went this far into the reality of history. At least with a precise date and page from Mark, she didn't have to spend so much time searching.

"Or a podcast." Satya's voice was an unexpected addition to their conversation.

"A what?" Mark, for once, didn't know what something modern was.

Chloe answered him. "Oh, it's sort of like radio, or news? Only most of them are regular people talking about topics. True crime, history, gardening, that sort of thing. I'll play some for you." Chloe thought about it. "I suppose that could be a reason, they were research material. But why send them all to me?"

"Have you asked him?"

Chloe narrowed her eyes at Mark. "Being all logical on me again? I tried email, but he didn't respond."

"Did you call him? Who is him?" Satya seemed to be invested in the project now, as well. Perhaps he thought he owed Chloe for her offer of a home. If you could call a vacant crypt a home.

"One of my teachers. *Former* teachers," she stressed. Getting out of school had been the most momentous thing in her life to date. (She did include near-death by spirit in that.) "I don't have a phone number. And now that I'm thinking of it, I'm not even sure he still teaches there, so I may not have a valid email. The return address on the package would be about it." She pulled out her phone. "I don't really want to visit him, not yet anyway. I'm just... awkward."

"No, visiting him is *not* a good idea." Mark's tone was quite firm. "You don't know what his interest in these women was. It would not be safe to go alone."

"And you can't come with me. Either of you." Chloe felt her throat tighten, and she flopped into a chair with a strangled noise. "All right. We have more work to do. I promised." She sat up straight and took the microfiche carefully. "I've got my part, and you can point me to the others as soon as..."

The ghosts went away, and she sat in front of the machine to get going on her research. It was some time later, and a small stack of printed sheets of paper later that she felt her phone buzzing. She pulled it out and looked at it, then put it away again.

"Time to catch the bus home." She stretched and yawned. "Mark, thank you. I think we've found enough to have a timeline, although I am not sure yet what it means. If it means anything."

"What are you going to do with this?" Satya was hovering near the door.

"Take it to my boss." Chloe scooped up the stack and shoved it into her bag. She was more careful repackaging the clippings. "Who may tell me what happens next, and may not. Honestly I'm not sure I want to know."

"Why?"

"He's... he's not creepy. Just, you know, not really of this world sometimes." She shrugged.

Mark offered. "Uncanny?"

"That's a good word." She waved, and he waved back. "Come on, Satya, I think I can smuggle you on the bus ride."

TRAVELING IN GHOSTS

Whatever Satya's motives in having been scary before, now he followed her meekly, like a scolded puppy. If he'd had a tail, it would have been drooping like his head was. He followed her in silence up the stairs, and out into the public area of the library. Chloe pulled the door marked 'authorized personnel only' closed behind her, scanning the big lobby as she did so. No one was looking at them. Even the librarian at the front desk was looking down at her computer, half hidden behind the tall counter where you'd put your books to check out, or return.

Chloe headed for the exit. She hadn't really thought about it before, but other than that first visit where she'd been ushered down to the archive room, they seemed to ignore her coming and going. Even the patrons paid no attention to her. She might as well have been a ghost herself.

It took no effort to smuggle Satya on the bus. She swiped her fare card, and walked to her usual place - the row second from the back of the bus. Satya, at her gesture, moved into the seat closest to the window. Chloe sat as she took off her backpack in a practiced move. She shoved the bag by her feet, not wanting to put it in the middle of her companion.

"It's a little weird to see you standing *in* the chair." She pointed out to him in a soft tone. Talking to oneself on the bus was *de rigeur*, it just meant she was less likely to be hassled. No point in getting herself thrown off, though, being loud.

"Yeah. I just can't seem to make myself fit to things, any more." He looked down at himself as though seeing his translucent state for the first time.

The bus was not a fast way to get home, but Chloe had refused to get a car, despite her mother's silent disapproval. She'd only reluctantly gotten her driver's license, hated driving, and living at her job, she really didn't need one. Only…there were times it would be very convenient to have a car and not be reliant on the vagaries of the bus. Like today.

"Why," Satya hissed in her ear, "is there an angel on the bus?"

Chloe bent over and dug in her bag for her headphones. She slid them on, and only then did she answer him in a low tone. Their fellow passengers could assume she was making a phone call. She rode this bus often enough to not want the crazy label slapped on her.

"It's CincyCon this weekend." She expected this to spark confusion, but he seemed to understand it. She revised her mental estimate of just how long he'd been dead. Or rather, how recently he'd left the living plane. She had questions that couldn't be voiced in public, not even on a pretend phone call.

The angel wasn't the only strangely dressed person on the bus now, as they were within a few stops of the big conference center where the convention was going on.

Chloe turned her head away from the ghost and looked out at the sidewalks thronged with people in various costumes and what she thought of as congarb.

Until the last year, her life had revolved around the three cons a year she did. Cosplay took a lot of time and effort, even with help. Since she'd gone to work at Belleview, the desire to be around her fellow geeks and nerds had faded. Nothing at the con could possibly compare to escorting a lost soul home to a sepulcher crowned with vaguely Minoan bulls. She'd looked them up. They were certainly not standard Christian imagery, unlike probably ninety percent of the other memorials in the cemetery. Not to mention that after she'd shown him to his new place, she intended to have a quiet word with her boss about him, and the results of her search at the library.

The bus lurched back into motion, much emptier now that the con stop was behind them. She looked at Satya, who was swaying beside her, mostly wispy pale. Her stomach growled.

"If you're feeding off me..." she muttered at him.

"No, no!" He flickered into near-solidity. "I'm not, honest."

"Then who?" She looked around the bus. There were three or four others, including a man slumped nearby, snoring. "Knock it off."

She hadn't had any idea before today that this was how it was done, but it explained a lot now that she did. She narrowed her eyes at Satya, who looked frightened and faded until he was a mere shimmer in the air. "That's better."

"How much longer?" he asked. She could hear him clearly, and now she was wondering how that worked. It wasn't sound waves, because no one else was hearing him, or seeing him.

"A while. Are you tied to a place and you can't go too far from it?"

"No, I told you I don't know where my grave is."

Chloe crossed her arms and leaned back, feigning a doze. She didn't want to keep talking to him. Not that a crazy woman on the bus was going to attract any more attention than any day that ended in Y. She had questions, for Mark about the whole grave thing, because this made it sound like he might be buried in the library or something. Only maybe that was private and she shouldn't ask Mark.

She really needed to have a long talk with her boss. First, though, she needed to settle the new occupant into Belleview. Which got her started thinking about introductions, and etiquette, and if she should have asked before assuming it was ok to move him into a vacant crypt. Would Mr. Cruor mind? She hoped not. She liked her boss, and by all evidence, he seemed to like and trust her. She had a feeling he was lonely, in spite of Della and Trunk the troll living in the big house. They weren't human, and did that make her... She shook her head, dissipating her thoughts. She really wasn't sure what the polite thing was to do in this case. And she couldn't ask anyone outside Belleview. That she was very sure about.

The bus stop wasn't at the cemetery entrance, of course. Who would need to come and go to the city of the dead inside the greater mass of the living? Not that the cemetery didn't hold its own community. Chloe got off the bus, seeing Satya moving in her wake like some kind of ectoplasmic shadow, and settled her backpack comfortably before turning to walk up the hill. Belleview had such a beautiful view, and took its name from it, for being in a location where building homes would have been awkward at best a hundred and fifty years earlier. The city was older than it, of course, but it dated to the first boom of the people who'd built here. The Ohio River had been the gateway to the frontier, back then. It all seemed a little unreal to Chloe as she trudged alongside the massive stone wall that completely encircled Belleview. She was walking on a crumbling sidewalk, picking her way around trash and things she tried not to look closely at. But inside the walls…

She picked up her pace a little as she got close to the entrance. The big iron gates were still open at this time of the day, so she made for them rather than the small iron-bound oak door where she could pass during the later hours when visiting was done. She was almost home. Her stomach growled, on cue, and she took a deep breath, promising it tea and then more solid substance. But first…

"I'm going to take you to your new digs." She spoke aloud to Satya for the first time since the bus.

"Thank you?" He sounded subdued and uncertain, a big change from the menacing ghost who'd tried to frighten her earlier in the day.

"You need a place?" Chloe wasn't about to offer to find his real grave, where his body lay. She'd been down that path before, and it had nearly ended in disaster. "I know of a place where no one's living."

"No one?" He repeated.

"Well, I don't think so. Never seen a ghost there, anyway. We don't have a lot of other things that live in the crypts around here." Other than Benny the ghoul, that was another factor. She should introduce them. Or not.

"I'm taking this," she announced, walking up to her beefed-up golf cart that was her primary workhorse for reaching deep into the cemetery with the tools of her trade.

Like the rakes and shovels neatly sticking up from the trash can strapped firmly to the back. This evening she wasn't taking it for that, it was just, "I'm tired and still have a meeting tonight."

Satya awkwardly tried to sit next to her, which ended with him sort of in the upholstery, like he was sticking out of a bog, but she didn't say anything to him as she pulled onto the main road through the cemetery. No point in embarrassing him when she could tell he was trying.

"This one is in a weird place." She didn't know why she felt she needed to explain. "I think it's the bulls."

He looked around. "This is much larger than I'd imagined it would be."

"It's bigger on the inside."

He flashed her a ghostly grin, managing to convey white teeth and amusement. "I understood that joke!"

"Um, well, it really isn't. But yeah, Belleview is pretty large. I don't know how many graves exactly. Thousands." She turned off onto a side route. He slid a few inches toward the far edge of the seat. "Er, I know buckling in won't help..."

"No." He repositioned. "I'm sorry."

She sighed out loud. "No, I'll warn you before I take a turn. Hopefully that will help. It's not like you can read my mind."

"I cannot do that." He sounded fervently relieved as he agreed.

"Turning left, now." She turned.

"That was not left!" He clung to one of the uprights, now.

"Oops. I have trouble with right and left sometimes. Anyway, we're almost there." She slowed the small vehicle to a stop, and Satya let go and drifted away from it before regaining his footing like he was still a human.

"I can't drive up," she pointed. "So from here I walk."

She started up the hill. They were under the crest of the hill, which was set aside for some truly monumental memorials, of the top families in the city, she'd surmised. Here, there were still some spectacular examples of sculpture and carving on some of the crypts. Like the one she was leading him towards. The interior was dry and empty. Before... before she'd learned not to, she'd peeked into it, curious, and other than a little pile of dead leaves in the far corner, it was seemingly completely empty. It was the four bulls, one on each corner, which had caught her attention about it. She looked up at them, now.

"It's different." She shrugged. "I liked how they almost look alive, and they have expressions."

One looked angry, but the others looked different, like they were waiting, or something. She'd never been able to figure it out. They all faced inward, across the flat top, at one another. You'd think they would be looking outward, guarding the contents of the memorial.

"Anyway." She cleared her throat after a long silence. "I'm going to have to meet with my boss now."

"Thanks. I appreciate you bringing me here."

"Er, do you... need anything?" Chloe shrugged. "I never know just what my job requires. I'm a caretaker, you see. I'm supposed to take care of... stuff."

"I don't know what to do now." He looked from her, to the partly-open door, and back again. "I guess I'll see you around?"

"Right. See you." Chloe turned and made her way back to her cart, moving slower than she'd have liked. But slipping and falling on her butt would only make this more weird than it already was.

DENIZENS

Back on her way again, she found that she was finally relaxing. She hadn't realized, until it was over, how much escorting Satya back to the cemetery had wound her up. She was even considering popping in to her apartment for a quick snack before meeting with Mr. Cruor to present her non-findings.

Which lasted until she pulled around the corner of the building, headed for the stables to park, and saw him standing on the steps looking for her.

"Hello!" Chloe waved. "Let me put this away, sir?"

"Go ahead." He leaned on the cane and watched her as she maneuvered into the shelter. "I hadn't seen you arrive," he spoke again as she walked up the steps towards him.

"I had something to do right away, sorry." She wasn't sure how to tell him about Satya, still.

"I'm sure you are quite capable of handling yourself, but I find I worry when you are off the grounds."

She met his pale-blue eyes, with their white brows arched slightly, and wriggled in discomfort. "It's fine, sir. I had... I don't know what to do..."

He tilted his head ever so slightly.

Her cheeks felt warm. "There was a ghost, you see. Not the ghost I was planning to meet..." She stopped and took a very deep breath. "Life is so complicated when I start saying this stuff out loud."

"It is complex even in silence, Miss Brandt, I assure you. I find that sometimes, speaking a problem can refine it into a semblance of understanding. Perhaps, though, tea would assist you in this?"

"Yes," Chloe didn't hesitate as she once would have. "Please."

"Very good. I took the liberty of having Miss Dear prepare a tray." He turned, and Chloe followed him towards the office door, rather than to the big door. She'd only used it once before, and that was a memory she could do without as well.

Della Dear was not in the office when they entered, but the steaming teapot spoke of her recent presence. The pile of sandwiches in a geometric design beside it was not something Chloe had seen her do before, though. As were the tiny, perfectly iced little cakes on a plate beside them. Her stomach growled enthusiastically and Mr. Cruor chuckled in response.

"I am glad to hear my instinct was correct, to provide for sustenance." He gestured. "Please sit and eat."

"Sir," Chloe took her usual seat in the upholstered chair, while he sat on the other side of the table. "This is..."

He interrupted her. "You are a modest and unassuming young woman, and I am assured that is rare and unusual of your generation. Observation, however, tells me it is thus in *any* generation. Your gratitude has been noted, however, you do need to eat, yes?"

"Yes, thank you." She accepted the plate he handed to her, with three delicate sandwiches on it. They had no crusts and looked... perfect. She decided she wasn't going to ask what the filling in them was. One was a pale orangey-yellow, another a sort of salmon pink, and the third a green that reminded her of matcha but probably wasn't.

"Two lumps, or three?" His thin hand, holding the silver tongs, was poised over her teacup.

"Two, thank you." She was hungry, but not in dire need of sugar.

The sandwiches were all savory, meaning the green one hadn't been tea flavored. Instead, she thought it had been a cheese and vegetable mixture. The salmon had been salmon, of course. The orange one had been cheese, she thought. Mr. Cruor had nibbled along with her, but it wasn't until she'd turned down yet another sandwich, while realizing that she'd eaten several, that he brought the conversation back to where they'd begun.

"Perhaps," he placed a little cake on another small plate. "The best way to begin is with the ending."

"Not at the beginning?" She took it and looked at the lavender color with a smile. Della had picked up on her favorites, somehow. The little crystallized violet on top was perfect. "Usually, that's where you do."

"I think in this case, the end. Since I already know the beginning."

"I brought a ghost home." Chloe looked down at her plate, frowning, but not really seeing the confection. "I mean... I didn't know why, but now I think I do."

"Really?" He had his hands steepled in front of him, in the way she'd learned to associate with intent listening.

"Well, he scared me. I mean he was *trying* to. It was how he was getting attention. But really he was scared, and... maybe here he'll learn how not to be so ghastly."

"So, a school for the newly dead?" His lips twitched.

"Not really. Simply that, well, my mother always told me you become like who you spend time with. And most of the, ah..."

"Denizens?" He murmured.

"Denizens of Belleview behave decently." She cut a little piece of the cake, curious to see what lay inside. It was two layers of a white sponge cake with a dark purple jammy filling in between. "At least, according to their rules."

"Indeed and that is not always the same code as our human world that surrounds them."

She thought about Benny. "Or maybe they are the same as they were when alive? And the polite ones don't haunt, or, er, invade your personal space?"

"A very interesting thought, that. You postulate a kind of limbo, until they have learned... something?"

The purple was very sweet and flowery. Chloe wondered what it was made of. "I don't know. I'm trying to make sense of it all. It's... there's a lot. Like why I went to the library today. Why did he send me all those clippings. Why me?"

"We can table the discussion of the reason for Belleview until later, although I will tell you the term for the concept is purgatory, albeit that is very theologically incorrect. As for the other... it ties into what you've been trying to do. To make some sense out of life, and find a reason for it all." He folded his hands on the table, one over the other. "I will caution you. Life does not *have* to make sense. Attempting to force it into a design very rarely leads you to truth. However, there are indeed patterns we can pick out of the noise. Signal, if you will, that can tell us stories. That, I suspect, is why you received that package of clues. He was unable to put them together and thought that you might be able to."

"Why *me*, though?" Chloe felt like throwing her hands in the air, but didn't, instead mimicking his gesture. She found it was calming to have her hands against the cool cloth on the table. "I wasn't a top student, you know. I was just there, until I'd done my time..."

"Like a prison?" He was back to the very quiet murmur she almost couldn't hear.

She ignored that. "I don't understand why he picked me."

"I can think of a couple of things." He spoke in a normal tone, and gestured towards the door. "For one thing, you consider the world as it comes to you, without setting your expectations over it, constraining what you see to what you want to see. I suspect he observed that quality in you, while he had you in his classroom."

Chloe shrugged. School had been a painfully boring blur. She had managed to get through it, and had adamantly refused to do it again. There was no college in her future.

Mr. Cruor went on, "Add to that the recent publicity, where you were portrayed, like it or not, as something of a girl detective in the media."

"I was not!" She meant her own actions, because he wasn't wrong about the newspaper.

"Finally, whether you realize it or not, Belleview has something of a reputation among certain elements. I have had to be quite firm with ghost hunters."

"Wait." Chloe held up a hand reflexively to stop him. "What? There were *whats*?"

His lips quirked upward, and there was a chuckle in his voice. "Not everyone maintains a staunch disbelief in the supernatural. Some even seek to profit from it."

"Oh, no." She buried her face in her hands. "The television show, right? Mark said something... at the library."

"I rather think they would not find what they were looking for, here at Belleview. Nor at the library." He shook his head. "Belleview exists in its present, er, form, as a sanctuary. One that is not meant for the living nor humans. Attracting attention is the last thing we want."

"And I brought in the police." Chloe wasn't about to feel regret for that. Those girls deserved better. They should have their own graves. "So I got attention, and now I've been given a mystery."

"You don't necessarily need to try and solve it," Mr. Cruor pointed out. "There was no plea with it. Just the clippings."

"I know. I mean... So Mark helped me with the research today. Before the other ghost showed up at the coffee shop."

His eyebrow arched. She sighed. "I told you it was complicated."

"No, that is simple enough. You were in need of sustenance. However, a haunted coffee shop seems..."

"Oh, he wasn't haunting the coffeeshop. He was in the lobby of the Beverly, and he was being seriously overdramatic, trying to get attention. Mark chased him, but he went in a place I couldn't go... and then he tracked us back to the library."

Her boss was frowning now. "I'm not at all happy with hearing he came after you."

"He was frightened, and lost, and I was the first living human to pay attention to him." She shrugged. "I know he's not from Belleview, but it seemed like the right thing to do was bring him back here. I hadn't thought about sanctuary, but I think I was feeling that."

"Very good. And you were able to date the clippings?"

She didn't think he was entirely comfortable with Satya's introduction, but she was game for changing the topic back to what this meeting was supposed to be about. Nothing had prepared her for a professional setting that included being fed fancy sandwiches, tea, and cakes.

"The oldest one is from 1899, and the newest is a month ago." She bent over and opened her bag to pull out the thick folder.

"And did you get an impression of anything else while you were researching?" He accepted the folder, but set it down on the table unopened, continuing to study her with those piercing blue eyes.

"Um," Chloe wasn't sure what he wanted.

"Chloe, you are an above-average intelligence with an off-kilter mind. As you went through all of the clippings, then the papers to find more information, what leapt out at you? Use your intuition here." He raised a single finger in admonition. "Not facts or figures. Simply the first thing in your mind."

"No one wanted them." She blurted, then felt her cheeks flush with heat. "I mean... there wasn't a lot of fuss in the clippings, or the papers. With most of them, they appeared once and that was it."

"Ah." Mr Cruor leaned back in his chair and smiled, faintly, at her. He had moved his hands off the table and out of sight. "This is significant."

"It is?" Chloe shook her head. "I mean, I guess if someone were taking them, they were looking for girls who no one would be looking for. Er. That sounds weird now that I say it out loud."

"It is, however, an astute observation. What is your other conclusion?"

"Other?" Chloe blinked. "Um."

"You have got to learn confidence in your presentation, child." He gave her a full smile, this time. "Come on, you said it already."

"I did?" Chloe thought about it. "Well, it's over too long a time span for it to have been Mr. Gray. Or any human, really. Wait. Is Mr. Gray not human?"

"I suspect you would have noticed. Humans are better at identifying non-human than they realize, even if they don't always put a name to it. The uncanny valley is a mighty chasm, and don't forget that just because you have a flexible mind, Chloe." He was very serious now. "Setting Mr. Gray aside, although I would dearly love to meet him and ask him questions, you have put your finger on it. If, and I stress *if*, all these news articles are connected, then something inhuman is behind it all. Which brings it into our realm, Miss Brandt."

"I'm not... Not qualified or anything." Chloe realized she had pushed herself back from the table and was making a warding gesture with both hands. "I really don't want to be involved."

"You are, simply by being here, and doing what you do," Mr. Cruor shook his head, looking mournful. "I never intended to bring you into danger, but here you are. I will not allow you to be unaware and unprepared. Therefore, part of your duties beginning..." He lifted his arm and glanced at his silver wristwatch, "tomorrow morning, is to become trained in basic self defense against the, er, other parts of your job." He looked at her with narrowed eyes. "I can only watch over you and guard you here. As today shows, all too clearly."

"Are you angry I brought home a ghost?" Chloe asked.

She was feeling more than a little overwhelmed at the moment.

"Not at all. You did just the right thing, in fact. I simply don't want to run any risks with you, child." He fell silent, looking at her. Chloe picked up her cup and drank the last of her tea, which had gone cold. "This is more complicated than you bargained for."

"Yes." She turned the cup around in her hands, carefully, looking at the bits of the leaves in the dregs of the tea. "But it's ok." She looked up and met his eyes. "It's interesting. I never know what to expect, and there are days where I think I wouldn't mind some boredom…"

He chuckled.

She went on. "And I think it's important. I never expected to have a job that mattered."

They looked at one another for a moment. Then, he nodded. "I never expected to have an apprentice. We have both found out much that is new. I am looking forward to learning with you, Miss Brandt."

He stood, and picked up the folder. "I am going to review this. Please take the remainder of the day off, you need to rest while you can. Tomorrow will be strenuous, mentally and physically. Please report here at eight sharp, and wear comfortable clothes you don't mind dirtying."

Chloe stood up. "Thank you, sir."

TEACHING MOMENT

Her little apartment over what had been the stables of the big mansion, and were now the garages, felt very empty. Chloe relaxed as soon as she locked the door behind her. Finally, a moment with no other people who needed her. She'd never realized, until she moved away from home and took this job, how nice it was to have her own refuge away from... anyone and everyone.

She'd just had tea, but more tea was always good, so she pressed the switch on her electric kettle as she headed for the bathroom, kicking off her shoes and shedding her hoodie as she went. Her apartment was bare-bones and she kept it tidy, but a little clutter happened from day to day. Some days, she was too tired to bother. Today, she'd take advantage of a half-day off to get it back to a baseline clean, if nothing else.

That, and she was going to take some time to veg out with a movie or a video game. She'd not realized how being an adult with capital A meant you had no time for yourself any more. If she did have time, she was making a meal, cleaning, or running an errand. Chloe made a face at her own reflection in the mirror. Riding the bus took forever. Her hair was holding the last dye, at least... she switched on the vanity lights and looked closely. The purple-black mixture was darker than her usual lavender or violet, and made her skin look paler than it's normal. Her eyebrows glinted with a little red, showing her true hair color. She'd learned the hard way to never try bleaching and dying them the exact shade as her hair.

The face in the mirror smirked a little at that memory. Fun hair color was one thing. Looking like a clown was another. She switched off the lights and could hear her kettle switch off a second later.

She was looking for a mug in the cupboard when she heard the knock at her door. Chloe took a deep breath and straightened her shoulders, then went to answer the door.

"Hello?" She opened the door and looked around, confused. There was no one on the small landing, and she didn't hear anyone on the stairs. She started to close the door and saw the small box lying on her mat.

Her mat didn't read 'welcome.' Her father had gotten it for her when she'd moved into the apartment, and it read 'Probably Not a Trap Door' on the rough fiber surface. The box was aligned perfectly over the word 'Trap.'

Chloe took a quick step back, then pulled out her cell phone and took a photo before she closed the door, with the box safely on the other side. Then she dialed the top number in her favorites.

Mr. Cruor answered, as he always did, before the second ring. "Belleview."

"Sir, there's a box on my mat." Chloe took a deep breath, stilling the shaking she didn't realize had started. "Someone rang the bell, but there was no-one there when I answered the door, and there's a box..."

"Stay where you are." He said. "Do not touch the box."

Chloe said "yes," before she realized she was talking to a dead line. She stood there staring at the wall for a moment before she shook her head and returned to make her abandoned tea. The water was more green-tea temperature than she wanted by then, so she turned the kettle back on, and prepared her mug with a tea ball of the loose stuff. This afternoon called for something stronger. As the kettle started burbling, she got another mug out of the cupboard for Mr. Cruor, should he want something. Her phone rang as she was pouring water into her own mug.

"Hello?" Chloe answered the unknown number hesitantly, then relaxed as her boss's familiar voice sounded in her ear.

"Could you please open your door? Don't come out, just open it."

She did as told, and was facing Mr. Cruor, who was

holding a sleek cell phone to his ear, a jarring incongruity. He hung up as soon as she opened the door. Chloe tucked her own phone into her pocket.

"Interesting placement," He pointed down at the box. "I have to think it was intentional."

"Someone has a terrible sense of humor." Chloe glared down at it.

"There is no address. Hm." He reached in his blazer pocket and pulled out a baggie of white powder. As Chloe watched, he pulled out a large pinch and scattered it over the box and her welcome mat. "Baking soda. Leaves less mess than flour, and the chemical reactivity... ah."

Chloe stared at the box. It didn't look like anything had happened to her. "Sir?"

"Step back, please. I'd prefer you close your door, but as you need to know how to do this, leave it open, putting most of your body behind it."

Chloe swung her door partly closed, feeling the weight of the steel in her hand. She'd never really thought about it's construction until now. Mr. Crour carefully hiked his pant legs and settled into a crouch, peering at the box. After a moment, he reached out and delicately lifted it up, raising it until he could look at the bottom of the box without tipping it over. Then, he stood, holding it in both hands.

"I am going to take this, carefully, into the driveway. Please accompany me."

Chloe followed him down the stairs, and out on the pavement until they were away from all the buildings. He set the box down on the ground, then looked at her.

"Have you perhaps got a bamboo pole, for trellising?"

Confused, Chloe blinked. It took her a moment to recall if she did, after the apparent non-sequitur. "Um. Yes, I do."

"Perfect. The longest you have, if you would?"

She trotted off towards the utility shed, and returned a few moments later with a ten foot pole.

"Ten feet is the longest I have," She was panting just a little from her hurry.

"So. I shall now touch the box with a ten-foot pole." His lips quirked.

"Oh. I see."

"Please keep your distance..." He waited for her to back away, then prodded the box until it turned over. Nothing happened.

"Ah, good. And now, let us look at the adhesive."

"Why?" Chloe had so many questions, but this was the first she'd felt confident enough to express.

"If it was a reused box, there may be traces that will enable us to ascertain it's origin. If it was freshly assembled, the same is true. Every detail is important, Chloe. Time taken to observe all that is possible, at each step of the investigation, is never time wasted."

Chloe realized her education was beginning now, rather than in the morning. The sun was starting to sink, and the light was golden on the little brown box. "Right. What are we looking for? It's the kind of brown paper tape I see all the time."

"Yes, it is. If it were clear packing tape, that would tell us something. As it would were it a sturdy gray duct tape, yes?"

Chloe thought about this, and nodded. "Duct tape can't be used if you are shipping something with the post office."

"Indeed. This paper tape is not something most people have in their homes. The odds are, this box is recycled from a previous use."

"I don't see a packing label on it."

"There is an origin barcode, here." He turned the box

and showed her the side of it. "And a rough patch on the cardboard indicates the removal of something applied to the outside, which might have been a label." He turned the box over, revealing what had been the top when she'd first seen it. "Now, what do you see?"

"Clear packing tape." She crouched down alongside him. "It doesn't match the other seam. And it's been folded over on one side, to leave a tab for easy pulling off the roll. I do that."

"Hm." He pulled a small pocketknife out, and flicked the blade open. "Once again, I must ask you to step back."

"Sir, if there's a danger, I'd like to..."

"Very noble. However, Miss Brandt, if you suffer some injury alongside me, who will call for help?"

"Oh." Chloe moved away several paces, and watched him slice deftly through the tape. He pulled the flaps up, and looked inside, then looked back at her.

"It is safe to approach."

"How do you know?" Chloe asked as she walked up to look over his shoulder.

"I recognize the handwriting." He stood up, and handed her the note that had been in the box. "I will say, this wasn't quite what I was expecting."

"It's... Why didn't he use an envelope?" Chloe scanned the brief note.

"He may not have one. You mentioned that you tab your tape, and I have to wonder if the tape is from your own stores." Mr. Cruor lifted an eyebrow. "It is rather formal of him, I will say. You have made an impression."

"I've mostly just tried to be polite to Benny." Chloe sighed. "He's..."

"He's a ghoul, with all the hygiene issues that implies. You not mentioning that to him, or acting like you notice it, most likely means a lot to him," her boss smiled. "Are you going to accept his invitation?"

"Yes, of course. I need to know what this is about. And," Chloe looked up at her boss. "Diplomatically tell him to stick around next time and not scare me half to death."

"It was a teaching moment." Mr. Cruor's face looked tired, for a moment, then smoothed out. "Would you like me to come along?"

"He doesn't say to come alone." Chloe looked at the note again.

"Which would have meant I'd insist on coming." Mr. Cruor nodded.

Chloe made a face. "If it's not an inconvenience, sir, I'd like your company. I don't know what Benny is up to, and I'd like to show you where I left Satya, I'd forgotten about him while we were talking about the research."

"I had not. I intended to pay him a visit this night. However, having an introduction is perhaps a better way to conduct that call."

"Drat. I left my tea behind." Chloe looked at the wall around the cemetery, the tree beyond it, and the sun setting into them. "It's getting late. Would you like tea?"

"I think perhaps that you should get some rest, and we will meet again at full dark." He looked at the sunset as well. "Perhaps two hours?"

"That will give me time to get some dinner."

"Miss Brandt?" His voice caught her as she turned to head back for her place, still holding the note. She stopped and looked up at him. "Very well done, for your first lesson. Please continue to be as cautious."

She nodded, gulped, and hurried for the stairs, suddenly feeling all the nerves in her body for the first time since she'd looked down at the box. She stepped carefully over the powder on her doorstep, and closed the door firmly behind her, reassured by the solid weight of the metal in it. Then, she leaned back against it, and let out a single hiccuping sob.

INTERVIEW WITH A GHOUL

Even with the night dark, the cemetery was never completely dark or quiet. The shrill calling of the cicadas resounded off every tree, it seemed, mixing with a more subtle chorus of frogs, birds, and crickets. A few yellow sodium street lights burned at major intersections while she drove Mr. Cruor in the cart towards Benny's crypt.

"Would you prefer we put more of the lights back into service, Miss Brandt?" He asked, looking around.

"I'm not out in the night most of the time." She pointed out. "And I don't like heights, or working with electric."

He chuckled. "I would not ask it of you, I was thinking this could be hired contractors."

Chloe squirmed, then blurted. "I don't like having outsiders in."

He looked squarely at her, and she did her best to keep her eyes on the road. They weren't moving fast, but she really hadn't meant to say that, and was wishing she didn't have to explain it now.

"I see." He didn't ask her for that explanation, and she felt her shoulders relax again.

"The crypt where I left Satya isn't far from the route to Benny's." Chloe said.

"And perhaps it would be best to make that detour before we tire." Mr. Cruor spoke aloud the rest of her thought, although she wouldn't have put it quite that way.

If he had, Chloe thought, she'd think he was reading her mind. As it was.

"Yes, sir." She slowed for a turn. "I'm usually in bed late, but if we meet Benny at midnight, well, he gets long-winded."

"I do recall." Mr. Cruor's murmur was hard to hear even over the quiet of the electric motor, and she found herself leaning in his direction. "I don't believe I have said that I appreciate your taking on the chore of being a listening ear for him."

"He's lonely." Chloe shrugged, and carefully made another turn. "We'll have to walk a bit, just up here."

"I'm not made of glass, young lady." His chuckle took the sting from his words. "All uphill, I suppose?"

"From here, yes." She stopped the little cart and put on the parking brake. The road was level enough, but still. She had a little anxiety about it suddenly rolling away from her.

"I do have a torch."

She half-expected fire on a stick, but instead he produced a sizable flashlight with a red light and a funny half-moon shield that made the light aim only at the ground in front of them. Chloe led the way, with him a half-pace behind and to her right.

The moon was rising over the crest of the hill as they neared the Minoan-looking crypt.

"Here we are. Don't those bulls look Minoan to you, sir?" Chloe pointed at the pale stone beasts above them, luminous in the moonshine.

"They do, because they are." He tilted the flashlight up and painted the lettering over the lintel in blood-warm light.

Chloe suppressed a shiver. The world was black and white and red, and she didn't like it.

"Sir Richard Deene," Mr. Cruor read, and then went on, "he was an early archeologist of the Minoan ruins. Desperately wanted to translate Linear A, and said that he had, but refused to show anyone his work. He was, poor chap, rather old and demented at that point. Anyway, he'd fled England over some controversy, and spent the last years of his life here of all places. The crypt was constructed during his lifetime to very exacting drawings. I can show them to you some day, if you like."

"I would like that." Chloe couldn't stop the shiver this time.

"And it's interesting you brought your stray ghost here." Mr. Cruor switched off his light, and the world went monochromatic. "Deene never haunted his own crypt. If he's anywhere, it's off in some ruins trying to find yet another clue. A Rosetta stone."

"Wouldn't he, er, have been able to ask? You know, after?"

She could see his face in the light, now, his eyes sunk into shadows. His eyebrow glinted silvery as he raised it. "The afterlife is far more complicated than that, Miss Brandt. As I suspect you may have begun to know."

"Well, yes. But does everyone have a ghost?"

"No," He shook his head emphatically. "Ghosts have many motivators, there are those who have left some great work unfinished, I think. Deene was likely one such."

He was silent for a moment, and they were inundated with the sounds of insect and bird life. There was no sign of Satya. She supposed he would show himself when he felt like it.

"We should get back to the cart." Chloe suggested. "If we want to be on time for Benny."

"Yes, of course. Punctuality is important, and one of

your strengths, Miss Brandt." Mr. Cruor shook himself slightly like a dog emerging from water. "Carry on."

Still moving carefully even with the moonlight, Chloe picked her way back down the hillside to where the cart stood waiting on them. She climbed in on her side, and her boss rocked the springs when he sat, bracing his cane between his knees. The flashlight had vanished again.

She turned the cart around at the next intersection, and headed back toward the main loop road, mindful of the time. The shadows danced in the moonlight as the breeze moved tree branches overhead. Neither of them spoke.

Benny's crypt, unlike the eerily beautiful Minoan decorated marble one they had just left, was ugly. It had always been ugly, Chloe had realized, looking at it in the daylight shortly after she'd met Benny. Constructed out of concrete, with crude, minimal decorations, the winters had not been kind to it. Spalled shards collected around the walls, and one corner of the roof looked as though something heavy had fallen on it. Since she had to weed whack around a large tree trunk nearby, she suspected the damage was related to the hollowed missing tree.

She stopped the cart, and looked around. There was no sign of the ghoul, and she couldn't smell him. There was a faint unpleasant odor, but it was more like he'd been there, not that he was presently inhabiting the same space as her.

"Miss Brandt?" Mr. Crour was holding out a very small blue jar to her. "A dab of this, on the upper lip beneath your nostrils may help."

She caught a potent whiff of wintergreen, and gingerly dabbed her fingertip into the ointment before doing as told. The smell was overpowering. A moment later she was glad of it, as Benny walked up beside her.

"Hello," he greeted them

"Hello Benny." Chloe responded.

"Ebenezer," Mr. Cruor nodded at the ghoul.

"Chloe, I thought you'd come by yourself." Benny shifted his weight from foot to foot. "This is... well, I guess it's sort of important but," he lowered his voice and leaned towards her, "I thought we'd make plans before you had to tell him."

"Then I am very glad I came along." Mr. Cruor stepped out of the cart as he spoke. "This will save time and possible misinterpretation. If it is an important matter regarding Belleview, I should be informed."

"Which is what I'd have told you," Chloe informed Benny.

He drooped. chastised. "Guess this is easier, yah."

Chloe waited, but he didn't immediately speak again, which was odd enough to make her start to wonder if the big undead dude was ok. Mr. Cruor, meanwhile, had walked around the cart and towards a bench that faced Benny's crypt. He pulled out a white handkerchief that caught the moonlight, and put it down on the dirty stone.

"Thought you might come in," Benny turned his face away from Chloe, his grayish skin not reflecting the light of the moon, but rather absorbing it into his matte black hair. He was clean shaven, something Chloe had wondered about. Did he have beard hair? Did he shave?

Mr. Cruor answered. "No thank you, Ebenezer. I have been in your home and do not care to repeat that experience. Nor shall I allow Chloe to subject herself to it. We shall conduct this interview here in the open air with the moon as our lamp."

Chloe got out of the cart and followed Benny towards her boss. She didn't have a nice handkerchief, but she also wasn't wearing a nice suit like Mr. Cruor was. With that in mind, she plopped down next to him and stared up at Benny.

Benny, in a weird twist, was even more nervous and twitchy than normal. He was practically bouncing from foot to foot. Other than his shifting, there was silence for a long, awkward time. Chloe opened her mouth to say something, anything. Mr. Cruor gently nudged her arm with his elbow, and when she looked at him, he shook his head very slightly. She closed her mouth again. Mr Cruor crossed his hands over the top of his cane, but otherwise he sat very upright and still.

"There's a part o'the cemetery's outside the walls," Benny blurted, finally, in a rush of words. His voice got louder as he kept speaking. "It's not right, all those not bein' cared for."

Chloe spoke at the same time as her boss.

"Outside the walls?"

"All those?"

They looked at one another. Benny, having delivered his message, settled on one foot like the heron who fished the ponds in the cemetery.

Chloe waited for Mr. Cruor. He lifted his hand to his face and gently pinched the bridge of his nose, his eyes closed. Then he folded his hands back neatly in his lap before opening his eyes.

"Benny, where is this 'part of the cemetery?'"

Chloe was impressed, she could hear the quote marks clearly in her boss's crystal-clear enunciation.

"I'll show you." Benny offered. He shifted to the other foot. "It's far, though."

Chloe blinked. "You can ride on the back of the side-by-side, I don't have a bin on there right now."

Both men looked at her, and she shrugged. "I'm not riding back there."

"Quite right," Mr. Cruor murmured. "However, before we go anywhere, I would like more details, Benny. Please begin at the beginning, when you learned about the outside-the-walls denizens."

Benny had opened his mouth at 'beginning' and then closed it again, as the clarification was added. His hands flapped a little at his sides, but he stayed on the same foot. "I heard them." He finally said. "I was patrolling," He paused and nodded at Chloe, "before you started here, and I liked to keep an eye on things, you know, because the deads stay put, but the lives, they ain't got no respect."

Mr. Cruor arched a thin eyebrow, but didn't say anything, and his eyes remained calm.

Benny went on, all in a rush. "I heard 'em moaning and thought it was lives, but then one of them came through the wall, looking confused. I asked her why she was away from her grave, and all she did was point back through the wall, and I could still hear them but she wasn't making a sound. Don't know why. Ghosts don't need a neck to talk with."

He ended on an aggrieved tone, and Chloe shivered at the mental image he'd given her.

"This was before Miss Brandt's tenure, and you said nothing?"

Benny shrugged.

"Why do you say that it's part of the cemetery?" Chloe asked.

"Cause there's dead people, like in here. More'n one. I can't go out there."

"Why now, Benny?" Mr. Cruor cut to the chase. "Why not before, or never?"

Benny shifted his feet. Both were on the ground, now. "She brought a new guy in. I figure if she's collectin' 'em, might as well make sure the outside one's are cared for, too."

Chloe found herself blinking in surprise yet again.

EXPLORATION

The next morning, Chloe slowed the utility vehicle to a stop. She and Mr. Crour sat in silence for a long moment. Benny, not the most agile ghoul, and Chloe had to stop and wonder if there were any agile ghouls, managed to get himself off the back of the little vehicle. Chloe didn't look back. The process of getting him on the small platform had been unpleasant to see. Some things she didn't want to repeat in her life.

He came around on Mr. Crour's side, slightly out of breath. Again, Chloe wondered why an undead creature would need breath. Was there a biological need for oxygen? What kept Benny animated, anyway?

"Right about there," Benny was pointing towards the tall stone wall. "That's where I saw her and heard the rest of them."

"I see." Mr. Crour's voice was very dry. "Thank you, Benny."

"Do you need me to walk you over there?" The ghoul sounded eager.

"No, I think we can take it from here." Mr Crour turned his head towards Chloe, dismissing the ghoul and addressing only her. "Miss Brandt, if you would please proceed to the Woodvine Road gate."

Chloe started up the quiet electric engine. If he wasn't going to ask Benny to climb back aboard, she wasn't going to stop and wait on the ghoul. Besides which, the gate was... visible from the outside, even if it shouldn't be open. It was a beautiful wrought iron with fleur de lis patterns. Painted a shiny black enamel with her own hands not a month before.

They drove in silence for a moment or two.

"This is not a road-legal vehicle." Mr. Crour startled her when he spoke. She had been contemplating the nature of life, and how a person could be both dead and very much alive and moving and thinking... well, ok, maybe not the brightest bulb, but still...

"No?" Chloe answered after a brief hesitation while her brain switched gears.

"So we will not drive it out onto the road."

"I hadn't planned on that, sir." She made a turn. They weren't far from Woodvine, now.

"However, there is an alley." He was leaning on his cane and looking off into the distance, slightly unfocused. Chloe glanced, then kept her own eyes on the narrow paved road that wound along parallel to the wall of the cemetery.

"There is?" She hadn't ventured far outside the gate, only to the edge of Woodvine to keep the shrubs trimmed and grass neatly mowed. It had been a weedy mess when she came to Belleview, but her priorities, self-imposed in lieu of any guidance from Mr. Cruor, had been to make the grounds tidy from the public areas inward. Keeping up appearances had seemed important.

"It will take us along the wall, behind the residences and their back gardens," Mr. Cruor put a hand into his pocket, leaning a little towards Chloe, who tried not to flinch at his sudden nearness. They stopped at the gate, and he handed her a ring of keys. "Do you need this?"

"No," She handed it back to him. "I have mine here."

She pulled her own ring, which wasn't nearly as big as his, out from its retractable leash clipped to her belt.

"Ah, good, I should never doubt your preparation." He waited in the cart while she unlocked the gate and pushed it open.

"I need to put a drop of oil on that again," she told him as she climbed back into the driver's seat. "And I wonder if there's a way to keep it from rusting so fast. I know I can't stop it rusting at all..."

"Miss Brandt, the weight of the world does not rest on your shoulders. Have you been taking the time to play, er..."

This was an old topic. "I have been playing my video games."

She turned the cart into the grassy little alley, which was barely recognizable as such. Only the fences cutting yards off short of it gave her a clue, and the faintly visible ruts where maintenance vehicles would travel a few times a year. Or, she mentally commented as Mr. Cruor ducked away from a bush that tried to come into the cart with them, perhaps less often than that.

Many of the houses on this street were abandoned, Chloe had noticed before, while working at keeping up the gate. Plywood, weathered into silvery streaked camouflage alongside the siding equally weathered and paintless, covered windows and doors.

"How will we know..." Chloe started to ask, when Mr. Cruor lifted his hand, palm towards her, as he looked out of his side of the cart at the backs of the houses. The wall of the cemetery loomed next to her side.

She stopped talking as soon as he gestured, and stopped the cart smoothly. Silence fell around them. It was eerily quiet, there in the tall grass with the overgrown shrubs pushing into the alley on both sides. The yard of the house they had stopped behind had been fenced, once upon a time, with a low picket fence. The bushes were a more effective privacy barrier than it would have been, even when it wasn't rotten and falling apart.

There weren't even insect noises. Chloe shivered.

Mr. Cruor pointed, soundlessly, and she followed the direction of his long, pale finger. A flicker of... something. The movement slipped from shadow to shadow, then vanished into the deep darkness of the open back door. But in the time it had to cross from shadows over the porch, Chloe had gotten a clear look at the thing. Too solid to be a ghost.

"What is it?" she murmured. Whispering, she'd been told once, made more noise than a low tone.

"Wraith." Mr. Crour matched her volume. "This is the place."

"Mmm..." Chloe hated to say it, "Sir?"

Now it was his turn to follow her point. There, in the shadows below a truly magnificent tulip tree which had shaded out all other vegetation, were gravestones. She wasn't sure how many, in the failing light, but they were clearly the arched marble oblongs of stone...

"Yes, this is the place." Mr. Crour picked up his cane and swung his legs out of the cart, standing slowly.

"Sir, maybe I should go..." Chloe hopped out and came around to his side before he'd made it more than a couple of slow, painful steps.

"Together, Miss Brandt," he replied, his tone firm. "If you would give me your arm?"

He'd never asked for her support before, but now Chloe held out her arm, and he put a hand on her forearm, hooked through her elbow, and she felt a slight weight. "More for my balance, I'm afraid this yard is full of tussocks," he explained. His cane in the other hand, they carefully made their way towards the big tree. "Have you got a flashlight?"

"I do. It's in that pocket, though."

They stopped at the edge of the shade, where the grass thinned and shortened into a more even layer underfoot, and he released her arm so she could retrieve the light. Chloe pulled out the stubby flashlight from her cargo pocket and turned it on.

A shaft of pure white light pierced the cavernous space beneath the tree's drooping protective branches. Close-up, Chloe could tell the scale of the stones.

"They are so little." She caught herself before her voice went up. "Tiny little stones. Not people sized."

"And the names," Mr Cruor had moved without her support, nearer to the stone closest. "Fido."

"Spot, Rex," she scanned the other stones. Some were unmarked, others crudely chiseled. "Bella."

"Pets, beloved of the family, yet kept from the big cemetery." Mr. Cruor stooped and took a look. "I wonder if the stonemason lived here. This is very good marble, and well shaped, which is not a trivial skill."

"Not all of them, though," Chloe pointed at markers further away, on the other side of the massive tree trunk. "Those look like wood. Or... Not sure what that was made out of, but not marble and maybe not even stone."

"The house has stood here, from the architecture, a century at least. Surely the same hand would not be employed to make each stone. And..." He paused.

"There are a lot of them." Chloe filled in.

"Indeed."

"Well, that was a red herring." She turned away from the miniature cemetery. "If I hadn't seen the wraith, I would have said Benny was being silly and playing a prank."

"No, this cannot be turned aside that lightly." He was looking in the same direction she was, now.

From this angle, the old house, silvered with weather and time, shrouded in the deep green of rampant vegetation, held its secrets well. She could see up onto the deep porch, now, but the light only went so far before it faded into shadows at the corner of the house. The windows seemed to be unbroken, but they reflected the merest glints of light as a breeze feathered through the shrubs.

"I don't know what to do," she said after a long moment.

"Perhaps we knock at the door. Would you prefer to wait with the cart?" He stepped out of the tree's shade and into the sunlight.

Chloe thought for a moment. "No."

"Taking care of me, now, are you?" He quirked his lips in a very slight smile.

"Yes." She squared her shoulders and stepped toward the porch with measured stride. "It's my job."

"I assure you..." He gave it up. "Thank you, Miss Brandt. Wholly unnecessary, but appreciated."

She went up the steps cautiously, worried the wood would not hold them. It did, although one step creaked loudly enough to announce them to any living inhabitants of the house. Once they were on the porch, she could see why the shadows were so deep at the corner of the house - the porch roof had collapsed there, and was hanging down from one corner until it touched the floorboards, which were also rotted and collapsing. The house smelled of wet leaves and mushrooms. A clean scent of decay, which she preferred over the other by far.

Mr. Cruor lifted one hand and rapped at the wooden door, ignoring that it was off a hinge and leaning drunkenly outward. Chloe couldn't see anything through the glass window in it, as the glass was coated with a thick haze of dirt and even a few wet leaves plastered on. She glanced to her right, at the big window, and caught a flicker of movement inside the house.

"There is someone in there." She blurted.

"Yes," He answered.

"We could just... go in." She was already reaching for the door. Not the handle, as there was no way it would swing on the remaining hinge, but the edge so she could lift it aside.

"No." He laid a hand on her arm very gently. "That could be unwise, Miss Brandt. We have not been invited."

"Um," She looked up at him, his pale face floating above his dark coat in the shadows. "Do we... need to be?"

He blinked. "No. However, if we go in, it is breaking and entering, even without the breaking part of that statute being strictly acted upon. Be patient."

Chloe settled back on her heels. "I'm sorry. I don't know what's gotten into me."

"I have... suspicions," he murmured, leaning towards the opening and peering into the house. "Hm. Yes."

"What is it?" She couldn't see past him.

"I think you are being called by the wraith," he answered, maneuvering his shoulders to keep her away from the door.

"I can't hear anything." She felt stupid as soon as she heard herself. "Oh. Should I leave?"

"Can you?"

She turned to get off the porch, and the movement in the window got her attention again. A pale face was pressed to the glass, showing an elegant curve of a jawline and a large, dark eye. A girl, perhaps her own age, radiantly ghostly.

"Mr. Cruor!" Chloe lifted her hand to point it out to him.

He caught her by the shoulders and firmly pushed her towards the steps. "Come on, then, time to go home."

"But, sir!" She twisted around, trying to get back to the door so she could talk to the ghost. "She might need me!"

"That depends on how you define need," he wasn't letting go, and she found that he was marching her down the steps, punctuated by the shriek of the wood rubbing when they stepped down onto the failing plank. "I also need you, and there are chores to be done, Miss Brandt. Come, come, time to go..." She stumbled on the rough lawn, and he held onto her, keeping her from falling. "Quickly, now!"

She'd never heard him raise his voice before, and it was that as much as the strength in his hands that propelled her towards their ride, faster than she meant to go, that kept her moving towards the cart.

He released her shoulders, and when she stopped, turning back to look behind them, he grabbed her hand.

There were wraiths coming out of the house. Wispy bundles of white smoke that was thickening into something like trailing dresses and long matted hair and deep shadowed places where faces ought to have been. Her fingers wrapped around his and she yielded, starting to run after him.

When they reached the cart she scrambled in, and fumbled in her pocket for the key, trying not to make visual connection - you couldn't call it eye contact - with the oncoming wraiths. They were moving slowly, now, as they reached the boundary of the lawn. She knew they could leave it, or they wouldn't have been able to encounter Benny, but...

Chloe put her foot down on the accelerator and twisted the wheel as hard as she could. There wasn't really enough room to make a full turn here, and she felt her throat tighten into choking pain of her terror tightening her muscles as she backed up from the bush she'd just driven them into, before she could finally go down the alley and away from the inexorable oncoming bevy of haunts.

"Why...?" She was clinging to the steering wheel as the cart bounced, moving faster than she usually asked it to go.

"Explanations later, Miss Brandt!" he shouted back, hanging on to the frame of the cart over his head.

DELLA SPEAKS

Chloe kept her foot hard on the pedal, accelerating recklessly, until they had popped out onto the street, and then had to brake sharply to make the turn into the narrow cemetery gate. Only once they were back inside the cemetery did she slow.

"Uh." She looked over at her boss. "What just happened?"

"Do you still feel a need to return to that house?"

She shook her head hard enough to whack herself in the face with her ponytail. "No. Not at all, in fact, never again."

"Good. Lock the gate, please."

She stopped the cart, then backed it up until she was close enough to walk back to the gate, cautiously. There was no urge to go beyond it, and she realized as she turned the key in the old lock that just this small action made her feel much better. An iron gate wouldn't stop a ghost, so what it was eluded her for the moment.

When she returned to Mr. Cruor, who had stayed quietly in the cart, he was looking past her, out through the iron swirls and motifs of the gate.

"They could come through the gate, right?"

"In theory." He kept his vigil, not looking at her while he talked to her. "Practically speaking, I don't think they will venture far from their nest. Please take us back to the main office, Miss Brandt."

Chloe, her legs feeling a little wobbly now that she was past whatever *that* had been, climbed back into the driver's seat. "Yes, sir."

They wound through the newer part of the cemetery, which meant the last grave had been dug and filled here perhaps fifty years before. This section still had regular visitors, so Chloe had focused her clean-up efforts on this part, the lowest part of the hilly terrain, when she had been hired. Her months of hard work had paid off with a much neater space around them. Gravestones stood in mowed, smooth green, instead of hidden beneath waves of prairie-like growth, and the shrubs had been cut back into a more controlled growth.

"You have done a very good job, Miss Brandt." Mr Cruor seemed to have shaken off the unpleasantness of the wraiths, and was now looking around with an expression of mild interest. "Working alone, which makes it all the more impressive."

"Um. Thank you?" Chloe wasn't sure what to say. She never knew how to respond to compliments. "It's what you hired me to do. I think…" She wasn't entirely certain, after the last few adventures.

"Oh, it was. However, I believe you will understand

when I say that I was unsure of your fitness for the position at first."

"I'm a girl," she shrugged.

"A young woman," he corrected gently, "and a very capable one. This would require a team, you realize, to fully maintain."

"I know." She let out a deep sigh. "It's not even close to what it should be, but at least you've given me all the equipment to make it easier."

"Less expensive than hiring unreliable workers," he pointed out. "Or risking insubordination that would have brought harm to you."

She blinked at the idea that he was worried about potential insults. "Oh, I have a pretty thick skin..."

"I didn't mean your feelings, Miss Brandt." He was looking at her, now. "I still need to teach you self-defense, and today has made that all the more apparent to me. We may have to hire in a crew to do the mowing and trimming for a while."

"What?" She was confused. A moment ago he'd been praising her and saying that hiring outsiders would be unreliable, hadn't he? "I can manage!"

"I am not slighting your work ethic. You cannot be in two places at once. Also, I hate to see your hard work go to waste and return to the wilderness while you are otherwise occupied."

They arrived in the big parking area by the funeral home. She pulled up at the office steps around to the side.

"It's ok..."

"No." He shook his head firmly, swinging his legs around and bracing with his cane to get out. "You have to learn how to keep yourself safe, and in doing so, to safeguard Belleview itself. And you still have much work to do on the old hilltop sections. I will hire a small crew to maintain what you have already done."

"I don't like the idea of outsiders, sir..." Chloe trailed him up the steps. He was moving slowly and carefully, as though he were in pain.

"Are you proposing that perhaps Benny could help?" He opened the door and gestured for her to precede him indoors.

"Well, no." Chloe didn't like to think of the ghoul with one of her precious lawn tractors. "Ok, I get that humans are the best option here. Just how much self-defense are you saying I'll need? And what about your duties?"

He limped past her, headed for the table in the center of the room. "I'll take care of those. I won't be your only trainer."

"Oh." Chloe joined him, sitting across the table from him. He hadn't done anything she could see to call Della, but the skeleton glided through the far doorway as Chloe took her own seat. Chloe smiled up at her, wondering if the Victorian-era housekeeper would be part of the training. Della, who couldn't show emotions through flesh and blood, nodded her head at the much younger woman. This, coming from her, was practically effusive.

"However, the first order of business needs to concern the wraith nest." Mr. Cruor looked up at Della. "Could you please ask Trunk to join us? And I will need you to sit in, as well."

Della nodded again, then silently went back the way she had come.

"A wraith nest? Is that what that was?" Chloe felt the hairs on her arms stand up. Whatever he called it, she didn't like it. She had not been in full control of herself, and that scared her more than anything else she'd encountered at Belleview.

"Yes." He looked at her, his eyes narrowed very slightly.

"How are wraiths different from ghosts?" she asked when he hadn't said anything for a long moment.

"Intent, partly, and power, mostly." He steepled his hands on the table in front of him. "What did you feel, while you were looking at the doorway?"

"I wanted to help her." Chloe shrugged. "I feel that way... not all the time, but a lot, since coming here and meeting different, er, denizens of Belleview. They have problems, and sometimes I can solve them. Like Satya."

"Hm. Yes. That would be very useful."

"What?" She was confused again, but the door had opened and a thud against the doorjamb had her spinning around to see what had made the noise.

Trunk ducked further, on his second attempt to come in the room, and made it through without further incident. Behind him, a clump of moss fell onto the floor from the doorway's edge, where it had been scraped off when he struck his head.

"Are you ok?" Chloe asked him.

The sound of falling gravel, Trunk's equivalent to a laugh, was his response. "Trunk have hard head."

"Yes, but still." She got up as he sank to a sitting position, his knees folded up in front of him. He was the reason there was a lot of open space in this room. Chairs and trolls didn't mix, so he would just take the floor during a meeting. "Let me look."

He smiled, the cleft rock planes of his face sliding grittily over one another, but bent his head so she could see the mark on it. "You worry about wood door, not me."

"Probably true. You've lost some moss. Hard to tell about the stone, you're chipped here."

He touched his own head gently. "Old dent. Not new."

Chloe retrieved the fallen moss, which was still moist, and patted it into place. "There."

"Thank you."

She sat down again, joining her boss and Della, who didn't sit. At all, that Chloe had ever seen.

"You have a compulsion, Miss Brandt," Mr. Cruor announced. "I begin to wonder if there is a geas involved."

"A geash? Gash?" She cocked her head. "I don't know that word."

"Ah. I shouldn't be surprised, and yet I am. A spell of compulsion, in essence."

Chloe shook her head, hard, once again. "No. Definitely not. I just like being helpful. And Trunk is my friend."

All three of them looked at her. Della didn't have eyebrows, but Mr. Cruor and Trunk both had theirs up, and Chloe was certain Della's invisible ones were somewhere on her brow, as well.

"He is." She crossed her arms. "Look, I know this is supposed to be a job, but, well, it's not a normal one."

"True," Mr. Cruor murmured.

"Trunk like Chloe, too." The troll was smiling again. "Chloe smart cookie, not crumbly."

Chloe giggled.

Mr. Cruor passed his hand over his face, hiding his eyes for a moment. When he uncovered them, he was frowning. "Miss Brandt, I apologize. The incident earlier shook me, and I am deeply concerned for you at this time."

Chloe opened her mouth to speak, and he held up a single finger to stop her.

"You are helpful. However, it can be taken advantage of,

and we will have to work on that. As Trunk has said, I think all of us are fond of you." He didn't pause, but both Della and Trunk nodded. "We desire nothing less than your wellbeing. However much you seem at times to be at cross purposes with that aim."

"What did I do?" Chloe felt her eyes get hot and wet. She took a deep breath. "Are you firing me?"

"No, Miss Brandt." His voice was very soft. "You are a valued member of the team. You frightened me today. Had I not been with you..." He took a deep breath.

"I'd have gone in there." Chloe blinked fast. "What would have happened?"

"I don't think you would have come out again."

Trunk rumbled. "Maybe tell us what happened?"

"Briefly, because at dusk we have much to do: there is a nest of wraiths in a house just outside the wall. They attempted to secure Miss Brandt to themselves for purposes I can only guess at, but none of my speculations are pleasant. We fled, but Miss Brandt has made a solid point which we can utilize to continue our inquiry."

"I did?" Chloe couldn't remember making any suggestions.

"You pointed out that Satya owes you a debt. Which means we can ask him to ask questions of the wraiths."

"Like what they were going to do with me?" Chloe shivered. "I don't want to go back there."

"And you shouldn't. Are you up to talking to Satya?"

"Who is Satya?" Trunk asked. He had wrapped his long arms around his knees and was watching them talk like a ball bouncing back and forth in front of him. Della tilted her head slightly towards Chloe.

"He's a ghost. I met him..." Chloe had to think. It had

been a long couple of days. "Yesterday, and he was lost, so I brought him to Belleview."

"You are tired." Mr. Cruor frowned.

"I'm fine. I can ask Satya to snoop around for us." She shook her head. "We don't have to wait until dark, I met him in daylight."

"It is easier to summon a reluctant ghost at night, however."

"You think he won't want to talk? He put in a lot of effort to get my attention," Chloe pointed out. "He seemed lonely."

"It's worth a try, but I was thinking that it is drawing near to the middle of the day, you have not eaten, and neither have I."

"Oh, I don't want to put Della to any trouble." Chloe clasped her hands together on her lap. "It's all right, I forget to eat all the time anyway."

Della leaned forward and picked up a pen from the center of the table, and pulled the notebook it had been on closer to the edge. Chloe watched, fascinated, as she wrote in very elegant script. The bones she was made of were dry and gleaming white, not a scrap of tendon remaining, but somehow she stayed together.

Della turned the notebook so Chloe could read what she had written. Chloe read it aloud for the benefit of Trunk and Mr. Cruor.

"You are no trouble, Miss Chloe, and I expect you to dinner at least thrice in a week."

Chloe looked up, and Della nodded firmly at her, before folding her bony hands at her waist and looking down at her. Chloe could almost picture the look of concern she'd have if she could.

"Della has spoken." Mr. Cruor's lips quirked as he spoke softly. "Well, then, we will sup before we hunt up a ghost."

LESSONS

It was past dusk when Chloe drove Mr. Cruor back into the cemetery proper, headed for the Minoan-inspired crypt where she had left Satya the ghost.

"What if he's not there?" She hadn't thought of that possibility until this very minute.

"Then we pursue other avenues." Mr. Crour radiated calm from his side of the cart. "In fact, that is a good first lesson for your self-defense training. There are always other options."

"What if you're in a corner?" Chloe flicked the headlights on, giving up her attempt to navigate by the light of the rising moon.

"Look up, or down. But primarily, do your very best to never be put into a corner."

"Hm." Chloe wasn't sure what to do about that. Her mind kept giving her unpleasant ways it could happen.

"Control of your surroundings begins by being aware of the situation, Miss Brandt."

"I suppose...." She looked around. "Is that why I don't like the headlights? They narrow my sight down to a tunnel of their lights."

"Quite likely."

"It's not like I have an alternative, though." Chloe shook her head. "Wait. Is there one?"

He surprised her with a small, dry chuckle. "There are several."

"I could drive with them off. If I went slow enough to see where I was going."

"You could use a different color headlamp," he suggested. "Red, while eerie, doesn't affect the night vision as much."

They had reached the hill and gone as far on wheels as was practical. Chloe put the little vehicle in park and switched off the headlights. The night looked very dark.

"Wait a moment," Mr. Cruor instructed. "Allow your eyes to adjust. This takes longer for some than it does others."

"Humans...?" Chloe bit off her question. She really didn't want to know what her boss was.

"Every individual is unique. Some have muscles that are a faster twitch reflex, and thereby adjust the irises and light access to the retina faster."

"I think I need to study anatomy." Chloe knew she sounded gloomy but couldn't help it. "This is going to be like going to school again, isn't it?"

"I certainly hope not." He got out on his side, and she realized that with the moon up, she could see fairly well. The world was black and white, with silvery highlights where the moonbeams fell.

Chloe led the way up the hill, trying not to move too fast. The shadows were tricky, and Mr. Cruor was leaning on his cane more than he usually did. Their adventure earlier had tired him out, and she felt guilty about it. They didn't talk until they had reached the crypt with its sharply-horned bulls outlined against the night sky.

Chloe couldn't quite make out the expression on Mr. Cruor's face, as his eyes had vanished into the shadows of his eyebrows. He remained silent, so she coughed to loosen her tight throat.

"Satya?" she called, raising her voice. "Satya, are you home?"

There was nothing, other than a distant owl's hoot in response to her voice. Chloe took a deep, slow breath.

"Satya, I need your help. You kinda owe me…"

"What do I owe you?" His voice came from the deepest shadows, under the portico of the crypt. "I don't owe you anything."

Chloe put her hands on her hips and face where the voice came from. "You scared me. I found you a place to stay. I think a small favor is a good exchange."

"What if I say no? Not like you can make me."

Now there was a small cough from Mr. Cruor. "A little matter of your actual grave, however…"

"You can't make me!" The ghost's tone was high and scared. Now, he was visible, a milky shimmer in the night.

"There are ways. A little dirt from the true grave…" Mr. Crour trailed off again, his voice diffident but not at all uncertain.

"What do you want?"

Satya was clear enough to see now, his arms wrapped around his thin body. He was wearing a tee shirt and jeans, or had been when he died. Chloe wasn't clear how that really worked, and wondered if ghosts could change clothes.

"I need you to go ask a few questions, then come back and tell me what you found out. It's like being a detective."

"I'm not real good with…" he struggled for the right word. "People."

"Not humans," Chloe clarified. "These are wraiths."

"Wait, aren't wraiths dangerous?"

Chloe found the idea of a ghost worrying about other ghosts funny, but tried not to show it.

Mr. Cruor answered in his slow, calm way. "Wraiths are

not dangerous to you. Very little can harm you, if you choose not to allow it."

"It would really help me out, Satya. You know what I was doing in the library today?"

He brightened, and not just in facial expression. "You were trying to figure out a mystery."

"Right, and this might be related to that." Chloe shrugged. "Or it might not. But it's my job to take care of the cemetery, and if part of it isn't in the right place, that's still something I need to know."

"Who's this, then?" Satya had come closer, and he gestured when he asked the question.

"My boss. It's important to him, too."

"What if the wraiths won't talk to me?" Satya was convinced, Chloe knew, at that point.

"They will," Mr. Crour assured the ghost. "You were lonely and sought out Chloe because she could see you. I think you will find that being seen, and listened to, is a need that persists past active living."

"I should just... listen?" He sounded unconvinced.

"Well, that would be a good place to start," Chloe took a breath, "and we have some questions for them."

They spent about an hour, with Mr. Crour moving over to a nearby bench and resting, going over what they wanted to know, until Satya had it all down and was confident that he wouldn't forget it.

"I'll be back tomorrow," Chloe promised.

"At dusk," Mr. Crour filled in. "Less energy for you, Satya."

Later, as they were driving back to the house, he told Chloe the rest of it. "You power him, in daylight, and it takes energy that you might not always have to give."

"Yeah," Chloe was thinking about Mark and his

attempts to lessen the draw on her. "Sometimes it's worth it, though."

"Conserve your resources, Miss Brandt. Lesson two. Always leave yourself a reservoir to draw on, against unexpected and needless to say, unpleasant surprises."

AN UNEXPECTED EMAIL

Chloe pressed the switch on her electric tea kettle and yawned, again. She'd slept far more soundly than she thought she would. The night before, as she dropped her boss off, he'd looked at her, leaning on his cane.

"Lesson three: sleep when you can."

"I don't think I'll be able to..." She was remembering the feeling of doing something she didn't want to do, but not even realizing she didn't want to be doing it until she was pulled away from it and kept safe in spite of herself. That was horrifying.

"Try, please. No computer or phone time. Sleepy tea, and warm blankets should do the trick."

She'd put her phone down on the little table when she'd come in, and hadn't turned on her computer. Now, she wandered over and booted it up, while her tea water was coming up to near-boiling. Not boiling hot, not for the tea she wanted to make, and it was worth the extra expense to have a tea kettle smart enough to let her choose the temp range. She picked up her phone and winced when she saw a stack of notification banners waiting. She put it right back down again.

"After tea," Chloe muttered to herself.

The kettle clicked off, and she poured the hot-but-not-boiling water over her leaves, enjoying the rush of fragrant steam from her mug. Picking it up, she carried it over to the computer desk and parked it on its coaster while she logged in to her email. She hadn't checked it at all the day before, and expected there would be more emails than she wanted to deal with, just like her phone notifications. The inbox scrolled automatically as new messages loaded, and she sat up very straight as she caught the subject line and sender of one in particular.

She opened it, scanned it, and hit the print button. Forgetting about the tea, she headed to get dressed. Mr. Crour needed to see this as soon as possible.

The morning air was chilly as she crossed the parking area to the big house, papers in one hand, and re-warmed tea mug in the other. He was usually up early, she knew, and hoped this morning would be no exception. Chloe let herself into the office, and got a surprised look from her boss as he turned to see who it was. He was sitting at his desk, wearing a long quilted jacket over his shirt and slacks. In a rare moment, she got to see him without a tie.

"Miss Brandt?" He rose as she walked towards him. "Is everything all right?"

"I don't know." She pushed the papers at him, and he accepted them without looking at them. "I didn't check my email yesterday..."

"Is that what this is?" Now he looked down at what she'd given him. "An email?"

"No, I mean, yes, but I printed it out for you since you don't do emails. I don't think. Do you?"

He didn't answer her question, instead murmuring while he read the email, "You do think, and far over what is necessary at times."

Chloe felt stung, and put her hands behind her back to clutch them together privately. He looked up at her, icy blue eyes piercing her subterfuge.

"I do have a computer. And overthinking is one of your few flaws. You are most valuable to me, Miss Brandt, never doubt that."

He looked back down at the paper, leaving her to wonder about the computer she'd never seen, what other office he might have, and how he'd realized she was upset. A few moments later he folded the pages up.

"May I keep this?" he asked. "Or perhaps, I should have you forward the email to me."

"I still can't wrap my head around you and a computer," Chloe blurted, then clapped a hand over her mouth.

He smiled and walked over to his desk, and from one of the drawers, produced a sleek laptop. "Voila!"

Chloe shook her head, smiling. Then she remembered what the email had been about and her smile dropped. "Why did he email me, then? Why not you?"

"At a guess, he has had your email since you were his student, and it has not changed...?" Mr. Crour elevated one eyebrow slightly in a gentle interrogative.

Chloe nodded, and he continued. "My email is published nowhere, known to very few, and my online presence, like the cemetery as a whole for that matter, is nonexistent. The same reasons he sent the clippings to you. Unless, of course, there is some unhealthy obsession with you, but I think the request to meet with me, rather than you alone, is reassuring there."

Chloe wrinkled her nose at the concept of her teacher... "Ew."

"Quite eloquent." After this dry rejoinder, Mr. Cruor looked at his watch. "Have you responded to him?"

"No. I wanted to talk to you first. And I didn't see that," she gestured in the general direction of the printed pages, "until late and I was tired. You said to sleep."

"Very good, you learned a lesson." He smiled. "Now, I said that self-defense lessons would begin today. Perhaps a practical application will be the best way to teach you."

"I don't do well in class." Chloe dropped her head. "I wasn't good at school."

"Nonsense. There are many ways to learn, and you were exposed to only one." Mr. Crour took a seat at his desk and pulled a black telephone with a dial from one of the cubbies normally hidden behind the roll top. He lifted the handle and started to rotate the dial.

Chloe knew she'd gone wide-eyed, but fortunately he was looking in the other direction and didn't see her face. She headed for her own desk while Mr. Crour was waiting. She could hear him clearly when the person on the other end of the connection answered.

"Good Morning, do I have the pleasure of speaking with Mr. Gray?"

Chloe couldn't, as hard as she tried, hear the other side of the conversation.

"It is rather unexpected, and yes, you did alarm Miss Brandt. However, we would like to meet with you in person. When would you be available today?"

Chloe stood up, with every intention of objecting to this arrangement. Mr. Crour didn't even turn his head, just dropped the pen he had been making notes with and lifted a finger in admonition. She subsided back into her chair.

"Excellent. We will see you then, please come to the side door, the front is so formal for this little gathering, I think."

And then, "Thank you, I will pass that on to her."

Mr. Crour set the telephone receiver back in it's cradle and made a final note before turning to meet Chloe's eyes.

She had her hands folded firmly in her lap, as a sort of way to remind herself to be still and quiet.

"The lesson for today is to meet on familiar ground. Whether you anticipate an enemy, or, perhaps, a friend." He paused. "Have you read Sun Tzu?"

"Sun who?" Chloe shook her head. "Mr. Gray is coming here?"

"For afternoon tea, yes. Which gives us time to work for a while before we see him. I would like to get his insight into his frankly rather peculiar behavior, and I would prefer that meeting be here, where we are in control of the situation."

"But..." Chloe trailed off and stared into space, her mind spinning through all the reasons having a perfectly mundane teacher come to her work was a very bad idea.

"He expressed concern over having upset you. He felt rather badly, as it had not evidently crossed his mind that you would not enjoy the little puzzle he'd sent you. He said to tell you he was bringing the drama llama with him." Mr. Crour's eyebrows were raised as high as Chloe had ever seen them.

Chloe felt a bubble of happiness pop in her chest, and she laughed. "He's bringing the Drama? Oh! I've missed that little guy!"

"Is this... an actual llama?" She'd succeeded in flustering her boss. Ghosts and ghouls and wraiths didn't do it, but livestock...

"No, it's a snake. A hognose snake. They are all about the drama, playing dead with flair when they feel threatened."

"A snake."

"He was the class pet," Chloe tried to explain.

Mr. Crour waved a hand. "You are the most extraordinary young woman."

"I'm really not. Snakes are just misunderstood," Chloe shrugged. "They don't want to hurt people, and they eat rats. Or mice, if they are as small as the Drama Llama."

"I can certainly appreciate that benefit of them." Mr Crour picked up his notes. "I did note that Mr. Gray seems to have more to say than his initial contact indicated. Which is another reason to have him here, where he can speak freely away from other ears as would be present at his workplace or in a public space."

"You think he knows..." Chloe's loose gesture indicated the cemetery, which her boss seemed to intuit.

"I suspect he has inklings. More people do than admit it, as you may have guessed."

"People seem to have a talent for only seeing what they want to." Chloe bit her lip. "Like being afraid of all snakes for no good reason."

"Ah," he leaned back and steepled his fingers in front of him, his eyes drifting nearly closed. "Much the same as people, in a general way, react to the undead. But there is good reason, Miss Brandt."

"Because their parents taught them to run and scream?" Chloe flushed. She really didn't like how snakes got a bad rap.

"In a sense, perhaps. Better to say that it's been taught since humans were human. From the first mother and father, to the first children."

"That's not a good reason." She folded her arms over her chest.

He chuckled, surprising her. "While no snakes bite for malevolent reasons, but to protect themselves or perhaps in a misguided attempt to secure food, spirits are not so simple and charmingly innocent, Miss Brandt."

"N-no, I see what you mean." She scrunched up her face in thought. "They are human, or human-like? Snakes are just creatures."

"Indeed. However, some are very dangerous. An instinct to hurl yourself away from them is most useful until you have a moment to identify the snake and determine if it can hurt you. If you go around picking up strange snakes...."

Chloe felt herself blush hotly, and he stopped, tilting his head slightly to one side. "Have you?"

"Um. Yes. I was mowing, and it was a very little snake..." She shrugged. "It wasn't venomous."

"Much becomes clear about you." He smiled and shook his head. "Most humans, who survived and perpetuated the human race, were much more cautious about snakes, and spirits. You and I are exceptional, which is not always a compliment. However, we are needed mediators." He lowered his hands to his knees and sat up very straight, looking into her eyes. "The spirit world is much more dangerous than your snake, and far more prone to drama and posturing, but unlike your small friend, there are *always* fangs hidden somewhere. Do keep that in mind."

Chloe nodded around a lump in her throat. Her boss dusted his empty hands together briskly. "Now, while I think you are a kinesthetic learner, there is some reading I will require of you. Please, make notes..."

Chloe turned obediently and got the journal from her desk. He'd given it to her when she started working for him, and she'd learned to write everything down. It really did help her to remember it even when she wasn't looking at the book.

Pen poised over page, she turned back to him and he started.

TEA AND TROUBLE

By two o'clock in the afternoon, Chloe was contemplating the change in her life. Sometime in the last couple of days, she and Mr. Crour had become less 'boss and employee' and more... something else. He'd called her his apprentice. He'd said they were mediators between the dead and the living. There was something stirring beneath the surface of her calm life mowing the lawn and she wasn't sure she liked it. It was not like she could say it was sudden. Just... she felt something had changed. It was unsettling. She found herself unable to concentrate on the book she was supposed to be reading. It was ancient, crumbling, and he'd given her cotton gloves to wear so she could turn the pages. He had also taught her how to do that, since it wasn't a normal book. She could believe that. It rested in a wooden stand specially built for very old books. Which meant she couldn't pick it up and pace with it, and she really needed to pace.

"Go outside, Miss Brandt." He didn't look up from his desk. "Do a few brisk laps and then, you will feel much better."

"I'm sorry, sir, I was trying..."

"Chloe." The use of her first name stunned her into silence. He put his glasses on the desk and contemplated her for a moment. "You need to walk. Best done out of doors. I promise we will talk this evening, but we have appointments with your Mr. Gray and then later, if you have not forgotten in the excitement, with Satya. We took a working lunch. I believe I have emphasized before that you must take time to relax."

"Exercise is relaxing?" she asked, but she was already standing up.

"Yes, it is. For the soul, if not the body. You need to move, so move."

Chloe left without further questioning.

After a couple of laps around the parking area she decided that she needed to be indoors when Mr. Gray arrived. She was fighting off anxiety as the time drew nearer to his appointment. When she walked into the office, Della was just setting out tea on the center table. The skeleton looked up and nodded at Chloe before making minor adjustments, then withdrawing noiselessly from the room.

"I wondered how that was going to work," Chloe spoke once Della had closed the door behind her.

"There are things I prefer not to put on display." Mr. Crour was standing by the tall bookshelves, an ordinary paperback in his hand. "Are you ready?"

"No." Chloe sat at her desk and stared at the small stack of books that hadn't been there when she left. "I need to read these?"

"Yes, but not today, and I think that you will enjoy some of them." He set the book he'd been holding down on the stack. "These are less about practical tactics and more about mindset."

"Oh." Chloe picked it up. "My parents have a bunch by this author."

"Excellent taste. I have pulled the books that have stories about the witches, and I do hope you will not model yourself after Nanny Ogg..."

The chime rang, interrupting them, and they both turned to look at the side door.

"I'll answer it," Chloe offered. She still had a sense of dread, but doing *something* would help ease her tension, she knew from past experience.

Mr. Crour followed more slowly. She arrived at the door as the person on the other side of it knocked, and she opened it to see the startled face of her former teacher, his hand still raised to strike the wood.

"Chloe?"

"Mr. Gray?"

They spoke at the same time, then stopped and just stared at one another for a second. Chloe knew he was seeing an oval, pale face framed in her long dark-purple hair, over a black tee shirt and grass-stained blue jeans. Not that much different from her school years. He, on the other side of the door, had changed so much she almost hadn't recognized him. Wouldn't have known it was him if she'd met him on the street. His hair was long, reaching past his shirt collar in wild gray elf-locks, and his beard was equally gray and untrimmed, until he had the effect of a ball of dirty wool wrapped around big dark-brown eyes. He was wearing a white button-down shirt that was badly wrinkled, untucked, over khaki slacks with… grass stains on the knees.

Chloe stepped back. "Er, this is Mr. Crour."

Her boss stepped forward, offering his hand.

Mr. Gray shifted the small animal carrier he'd been holding in the hand that wasn't occupied with beating on the door, and shook hands awkwardly.

"Hi, I'm, ah…" He shot a glance at Chloe, and finally finished. "Dave Gray."

"Please, come in. We will have a conversation over tea."

Mr. Crour gestured towards the laden table in the middle of the room.

Mr. Gray looked past them for the first time, and Chloe got to see his eyes widen. He took a couple of steps into the office, then turned and thrust the carrier towards Chloe. "Brought The Drama." He blurted.

She blinked, and took the carrier from him without thinking, and only then catching a faint whiff of snake musk. A big smile came over her face.

"Thank you, I missed him."

"He's yours. Can't keep him myself."

Chloe blinked in surprise, "I thought he was a classroom snake."

"He was, but I'm not... I'm not teaching any more."

That shouldn't have surprised her, given his wild appearance, but she felt her jaw drop open. "You're not?"

He shook his head, then looked over his shoulder at the tea table. "Um, this is... unexpected."

Chloe collected herself. This wasn't a reunion. Mr. Gray had wanted to meet her boss, or at least whoever was in charge of the cemetery, and had used her as a connection to accomplish this.

"Please, have a seat." Mr. Cruor pulled a chair slightly out. "Chloe?"

She sat, feeling a little awkward not only from the unfamiliar action of having her chair held for her, but also, doing that in front of Mr. Gray.

"Thank you." Mr Gray sat with a thump, like his energy had left him. Chloe set the snake carrier down on the other side of her seat, almost under the edge of the table. Mr. Crour sat across the table, facing her. "I didn't expect..."

"I find that food and drink are excellent social lubricants," Mr. Crour lifted the teapot, which was decorated in violets the color of Chloe's hair. "Do you drink tea, or perhaps coffee?"

"I do drink tea." Mr. Gray watched Mr. Crour pour out three cups of the warm brown liquid.

Chloe accepted hers, and reached for the sugar tongs while Mr. Gray received his cup. She took her customary three cubes, and passed the sugar. Mr. Gray was watching her, which made her feel very self conscious as she poured just a dollop of cream into her cup. Mr. Crour sipped his black.

"This is beautiful. I had no idea, Chloe." Mr. Gray had added a single sugar cube, and a good amount of cream, before he took his first sip. "I don't know what I expected, but it wasn't this."

"I like my job." Chloe answered. She had put some of the sandwiches on her plate, and now passed the tongs to him. "I didn't expect it to come with High Tea, either, but here we are."

Mr. Crour smiled. "Had you been a different person, it would not. However, while we are surprising you, Mr. Gray, you have surprised us, and we hope that you can enlighten us."

"The missing girls." Mr. Gray looked down at his plate, frowning. "It's really difficult to explain, and frankly sounds insane when I put it all in one place. It's... I sent the clippings because I thought that would be enough."

"What were you expecting?" Mr. Crour prompted gently. "That your concerns would ease?"

"There have been so many of them. And there's nothing. No bodies, no traces, just mysterious disappearances. I know, I know, people run away, bad things...." He looked briefly at Chloe and seemed to change the last two words as he said them. "They happen. You know that."

"Well,..." Chloe wasn't sure what she couldn't talk about. "Yes."

"We have researched the newspapers, Mr. Gray, and the disappearances you reference have happened over the course of a century or more. Just what is it you hoped to gain from bringing them to our attention?"

There was a long pause. Chloe couldn't tell what her former teacher was thinking, as he was still looking down at his plate, which held two untouched sandwich triangles, and his hair covered his eyes from this angle.

"This is... a cemetery. Where bodies are found." His voice was very soft.

"Indeed. And yes, two were found recently which did not come here by licit mechanisms."

Mr. Crour's vocabulary, Chloe knew, got more obscure when he was under some stress. She held her tongue and waited.

"Yes, that's partly it." Mr. Gray lifted his head and looked directly into Mr. Crour's eyes. "It's an old place, and begging your pardon, not, ah, kept up."

"Miss Brandt does her best, but she is only one woman." Mr. Crour nodded at her. "I can see what you are thinking. It is unlikely, for reasons, that a large number of illicit burials could have taken place here at Belleview. However, in light of recent events, you are correct that the number is not zero."

For some reason this made Mr. Gray sag back in his chair. "So. It might be..."

"No." Mr. Crour raised his finger in the way he usually stopped Chloe from her wilder speculations. "The earlier the disappearances, the more unlikely that they would have ended up here. Belleview was impeccably maintained, and there was a staff of twenty."

"Oh."

Chloe opened her mouth to blurt out something about the wraith nest, then shut it again. She picked up a sandwich and took a big bite to keep herself from saying something stupid. Mr. Crour caught it, she could tell, but Mr. Gray wasn't paying any attention to her any more.

"There's something else..." He trailed off, and Mr. Crour waited patiently for him. He poured himself another cup of tea, and added some to Mr. Gray's cup. "I had an experience."

"Oh?" Mr. Crour was noncommittal.

"I did.. I do, urbex. Which is, ah, exploring abandoned buildings in a city. For me, it's a beautiful and stark realization of the ephemeral reality of human hubris." Mr. Gray shrugged. "I'm a photographer, and capturing the way nature reclaims what we humans have discarded is a way for me to, I don't know."

"You find meaning in it." Mr. Crour put his cup down. "And you found something else."

"I found a ghost." Mr. Gray was sitting up very straight. "I can't explain it any other way. There was a presence, and it led me to a skeleton. Just... lying there. Like someone had gone to sleep and melted away."

"I see." Mr. Crour tilted his head very slightly to one side, and Chloe saw his eyes narrow. "Did you report your find?"

Mr. Gray shook his head. "I was trespassing, and I was a teacher. I didn't dare."

"Then why..."

"I started thinking about disappearing people, and how many there are, and how few are missed, and looked for. This one, the one I'd seen, it was in an old sleeping bag. The roof was partly fallen on it, and it had to have been there for years and years, and no-one had come looking for him, or her."

Chloe took another big bite of her sandwich, and while Mr. Gray looked down at his plate, picked up a piece of sandwich, then put it down again, Mr. Crour gave her a small nod.

"There are so many of them." Mr. Gray kept talking. "Year after year, and I keep seeing their faces in my dreams, when I sleep, which isn't much any more. I don't know what I had hoped that sending them to you would accomplish. I... didn't expect this." He picked the sandwich up again and this time he took a bite.

"I don't know that we can help you, I am sorry." Mr. Crour put his cup down. He steepled his fingers and leaned back in his chair. "You told Miss Brandt that you are no longer teaching."

"That's correct. I lost my job," his voice turned bitter, "due to having what they called a psychotic break."

Mr. Crour nodded. "You were seeing ghosts."

"I don't know!" Mr. Gray dropped his food, and buried his head in his hands, threading his thick fingers through his wild hair. "I have no idea." His voice was muffled.

"Sending the clippings to your former pupil was an act of desperation." Mr. Crour noted calmly. "One that did not stop the auditory and visual hallucinations. Did you do that before, or after you had been evaluated."

Mr. Gray didn't lift his head. "After."

"You thought it couldn't hurt, at that point, even if Miss Brandt took it in the wrong way."

"I didn't want to hurt Chloe." Mr. Gray lifted his face up and looked at her, eyes bloodshot and watering. "I wouldn't hurt you. You are just so... grounded. I thought you'd show them to him, and maybe..."

"She did. And we discreetly attempted to make sense of them. Which we are still doing."

Now it was Chloe's turn to cock her head in confusion at her boss. She didn't know everything he did, of course, but she hadn't been involved in.. no, the wraiths. There had to be bodies, somewhere. She blinked as a thought came to her.

"Mr. Gray," her boss spoke, rising to his feet. "We cannot help you, I am afraid. You should seek professional medical help. However, we will do our best to find your girls and help them rest."

"Thank you." Mr. Gray lurched to his feet. "That's all I can ask, is for someone to try. I can't, I *can't do anything*."

"You need to get help." Mr. Crour took his arm, gently, and guided him towards the door. "Did you drive yourself here?"

"No. Took the bus. I can't... I can't drive, my license..."

Mr. Crour looked over his shoulder at Chloe, who was standing by the table uncertain of whether to follow them.. "Please call an Uber for Mr. Gray."

They left through the door, then, and the way that her boss closed it behind him told Chloe to stay put, safely indoors. She made the call.

INVISIBLE WOUNDS

"What was that?" Chloe stood up as Mr. Crour came inside quietly. Had she not been watching the door, she wouldn't have heard him. "I didn't even know what to tell the Uber for a destination."

"That was a man at his breaking point," Mr. Crour told her, sadness in his voice and posture. "I sent him to the hospital."

"Oh." Chloe sat back down, heavily, and remembered how Mr. Gray had collapsed at the tea table not long before. "Why... What..."

She sputtered to a stop, and Mr. Crour joined her at the table. Della came up behind Chloe and made the young woman startle into a jump.

"Della, more tea, I think." Mr. Crour asked, "and unless Miss Brandt is hungry...?"

Chloe shook her head. Della started to clear the table onto her tea trolley. Mr. Crour leaned back, his eyes mostly closed. Chloe held her peace, waiting. There were times to talk, she was learning, and times to be silent and think.

When Mr. Crour opened his eyes and studied her face, she sat still.

"What are you thinking?" he finally asked.

"The wraith nest," Chloe told him honestly.

One of his eyebrows quirked upwards.

"Mr. Gray is really sick." She shrugged with one shoulder. "I don't know if he was really seeing ghosts. I don't know enough to have an opinion there, and I can't worry about him, because there's nothing I can do for him."

"Moderately incorrect, but go on." Mr. Crour's murmur didn't stem her need to talk.

"Well, you saw how it affected me. And it didn't affect you... did it?"

Mr. Crour shook his head.

"What if other girls, women, whatever, got close to it?"

"Perhaps. Think about the practical aspects."

Della came back with fresh tea, and Chloe used the lull to think. She looked up as Della placed a cup in front of her.

"Thank you, Della." She reached for the sugar cubes, which had somehow made their way back to her again. "What if..."

"A very good question," Mr. Crour interrupted her with a wry question. "Think about the timeline, Miss Brandt."

She blinked at him. "A century ago..."

"This was an upper class neighborhood. The wealthy tradesmen made their homes here."

"Oh."

"How would bodies have gone unnoticed, unlike the poor soul who so disturbed your Mr. Gray?"

"They wouldn't. What are we going to do about that skeleton?"

"We are not the caretakers for the dead of the city, Miss Brandt." He cradled his teacup and sighed just a little. "Even if I knew where it was, there is nothing we could directly do. An anonymous tip, and the proper authorities might take it from there."

"He would remember that, wouldn't he?"

"His mind is deeply fractured at this time. Perhaps, if he is able to mend and heal."

"What happened to him?"

"Ah." Mr. Crour set his cup down, and leaned forward, looking into her eyes. "Once, a long time ago, it was accepted that alongside the physical harm a man can feel, there is also what was called a moral injury. The current science does not accept this as a mental illness, in the way they do post-traumatic stress, but the depth of a moral wound is no less shallow, Miss Brandt. In fact, a physical injury may be more readily overcome than one of the psyche alone."

"I... I'm not sure I understand. Did finding the skeleton do that to him?"

"It may have been part of it. There was more to his story than he told us, I am certain."

"The missing women?" Chloe looked into her teacup,

and then reached for the teapot. "Are they really... no, I saw the news reports."

"They may not be connected," Mr. Crour pointed out. "Some of them may have left on their own, or come home again, which would be unlikely to make the news. However, some of them likely are connected, and your instincts are sound. The wraiths are a symptom of something deeply and profoundly wrong with that house."

"I wonder if Satya will have anything to tell us tonight." Chloe took a long, deep breath, then let it out slowly. "The little headstones. What if they aren't for pets?"

"It would be difficult, but not impossible, to bury that many in a yard." He shrugged. "The mechanisms of death are more my purview than yours, I understand. Suffice it to say that the tree would be an impediment."

"Roots." Chloe nodded, back into a topic that she understood. "So maybe they aren't buried there, but the stones are to mark... that they ended there."

"Perhaps. We cannot speculate too far afield. We can continue the investigation we have begun. However, remember that we cannot always know the whole story."

"Like the skulls." She nodded again, thinking about the strange case of the hoodoo votives that had come to them not long before. "We won't know what happened to them, before they died, or how they died, or where they went after the police took them."

"Correct. Our role is mediation, and as a bridge we cannot know the whole journey. Only to help from one place to another."

"This is what you want me to learn?" Chloe hunched her shoulders. "I don't know. I'm just... me. I mow grass."

"And swing a mean machete." His lips twitched into a smile, reflected in his eyes. "Your practicality is what makes you so effective, Miss Brandt. You don't get wrapped up in the existential dread and lose your way."

"Like Mr. Gray has."

"Yes."

They sat in silence for a while, the clock ticking in the niche between the doors the only sound in the room. Chloe sipped her tea, which was not as sweet, as she hadn't added more sugar with the last pour. It was lukewarm. They had been talking longer than she realized.

Mr. Crour broke the silence. "You should take care of your pet, Miss Brandt, before nightfall."

Chloe startled, then looked down at the carrier she had forgotten in the tension of the interview with her former science teacher. "I... is it ok I have a snake?"

"Why not?" He smiled. "There are warmer companions, but being too much alone is not good, Miss Brandt. I think he will give you someone to care for. However, I am unfamiliar with the care and feeding of... hognose, did you say?"

"Yes. I will need to get a vivarium set up for him. He can't stay in the carrier long. I wonder if he's been fed?"

"Go home for a little, Miss Brandt. See to his needs, and your own. I will see you at twilight." He rose from his chair, and she picked up the carrier.

"Ok, but if I have to go off in the bus to get things for him.."

"Ah, yes. That will take considerable time." Mr. Crour lifted his arm and looked at his silver watch. "I will meet you by the garage in an hour, then. We should have time for a quick trip, if you have a list and a plan for a single store. Tomorrow, perhaps, we can do more shopping for, er, the Drama Llama."

"Sir?" Chloe froze.

"Yes?"

"You don't have to…"

"Nonsense. I would do the same for Della or Trunk, who are *not* pets, but cannot go out on their own. And you don't drive. We care for those who are dependent on us, Miss Brandt. You know that."

"Yes, I do."

UNSPOKEN

Chloe pulled the utility vehicle around by the side door. Mr. Crour was waiting there for her, a pale figure in his gray coat and slacks against the dark building. They were later than they had planned to be, and it was fully dark. Only the lights of the city still glowed low in the sky, and the brightest stars were already twinkling overhead.

"Shall I turn off the headlights?" she asked as he took his seat.

"I don't think that is necessary on this trip."

She started off, then, slowly building speed as they turned out of the parking area and onto the narrow road of the cemetery. Chloe didn't feel like talking. They had talked mostly of snakes and their care, during the expedition to secure supplies for her new pet. She was still trying to digest the conversation with Mr. Gray and what that might mean.

"Are you lost in thought, Miss Brandt?"

Her boss sounded concerned.

"I'm trying to recalibrate," Chloe shrugged, then realized he probably couldn't see that. "Today was a lot, sir."

"Yes, it was. I find I am glad that you encountered this while with me, and sorry that you had to see it at all."

"I've met crazy people before. I mean, not over tea. Or

that I really knew. Just, you know, mostly on the bus." She made the turn slowly.

"Indeed. Which is not at all the same, and you know it."

"I guess so. I mostly tried to avoid them. Mr. Gray, I wanted to help."

"Understandably so. You also intuitively understood that talking to him of wraiths and ghosts would not help him, which was wise of you."

"I was watching you," she admitted. "You weren't saying anything, so I kept my mouth shut too."

"Trusting your instincts is a good thing, Miss Brandt."

She stopped the cart and put it into park. "This is going to be a bit tricky in the dark."

"I have my torch with me."

"Why do you call it that? I keep expecting a stick with fire on it when you do." She came around the nose of the cart, her eyes adjusting as she'd switched off the headlights and it was now fully dark.

He huffed a short laugh, and there was a beam of light from where he stood. "I forget that we sometimes speak different languages. I have a flashlight, but grew up calling it a torch."

She'd never heard him refer to his childhood before. She decided not to ask for more information. Not now.

"Slow and steady," he said, starting up the hill ahead of her. "There's no rush tonight."

"No, I guess there isn't." Chloe kept her light focused just behind his feet, keeping a good distance between them. "There isn't much we can do, is there?"

"There is," his feet stopped moving, and he turned, keeping his light low. "Don't feel that what you are doing is insignificant, Miss Brandt. You gave Mr. Gray a focus to work through some of his fears. He told me that having seen where you were helpful before gave him hope that we could resolve the mystery. That hope is enough. Solving the mystery is not the resolution he needed. Hope was, and is."

"Yes?" Chloe wasn't sure of that. Surely, having answers to the questions would be better.

"Much of life has no immediate meaning and purpose. We make those things as we look backward, not in the moment. In the moment, we simply try to do our job and survive. It's only later the ramifications become apparent."

"I just want to help." Chloe took a deep breath and then let it out again.

"You helped me."

Satya's voice, coming from the approximate range and location of her elbow, surprised Chloe enough that she actually jumped off the ground, and dropped her flashlight.

"She has good instincts," Mr. Crour sounded amused, and he shone his light on hers, as she bent to pick it up. "Hello, Satya. I apologize for our lateness."

"I was wondering if you had forgotten me." The ghost's voice was petulant. "But then I heard you coming."

"And you came to meet us, thank you." Mr. Crour was being very patient.

Chloe bit back yet another accusation that Satya has scared her again. He had, but it wouldn't help any of them for her to say it.

"I wanted to talk about... that place."

"The wraith nest?" Chloe asked.

"Shh!" Satya's voice got closer. "They might hear."

"They aren't anywhere close," Mr. Crour broke in. "What did you learn, Satya?"

"That harpies are real." He was speaking softly, and very quickly. "They hunger. They swirled all around me, then they left me alone when they realized I was like them.

But I could feel it, they are angry and sad and very, very hungry."

"Interesting." Mr. Crour sounded very calm, almost detached.

Chloe shone her light on the ground in front of her. She couldn't see Satya at all, only hear him.

"Did they speak to you?" Mr. Crour asked.

"No, but I could feel them," Satya repeated. "Inhuman. There were no voices, only wailing."

"Did you speak to them?"

Chloe wondered how Satya would react to the interrogation. If anything, he seemed to be relaxing, speaking more slowly.

"I asked who they were, like you said to." Satya paused. "That's when they swarmed me. But they didn't answer me."

"Did they show you their graves?"

Chloe wondered how and why they would have done that, if they hadn't even bothered to give away their names. There was a long silence, and she wondered if Satya had left.

"Yes." His voice was very soft, and she strained to hear it in the dark. Why would it be harder to hear when she couldn't see? She wondered. "They lie under the big tree."

"Thank you, Satya." Mr. Crour bowed slightly, Chloe could see him in the lights. "We are grateful for your assistance."

"They kill." Satya wasn't done. "They kill when they can. There are others, below the house. They lured them in to join in the lonely desolation of their own deaths."

"I thought you said they didn't talk to you," Chloe blurted out.

"They wouldn't have needed to talk," Mr. Crour answered her. "The dead need no voice to communicate."

"Oh." Chloe turned her head. "Sorry, Satya."

"You couldn't know." He spoke from the darkness. "I missed talking. I missed it so much. That's why, when I saw you..."

"But why did you scare me?" she asked him.

"Fear is a very loud emotion." Mr. Crour answered instead. "I suspect Satya had some small success with it before he encountered you."

"You were the only one who *talked* to me, though." Satya didn't answer Mr. Crour's guess.

"Are they the missing girls?" Chloe asked. She needed to know.

"They are all female."

"He wouldn't know that much, Miss Brandt. That you will have to wait on the news for."

"On the news?" Chloe was confused.

"An anonymous tip will be made, regarding the abandoned house, with a hint that perhaps the entire lot should be surveyed. It will not be a fast process, but in a year, perhaps two, you may have your answers."

"That sucks." Chloe felt angry suddenly. "That's too long!"

"It has been a century, if not more, for some of them. And they will not have begun with the wraiths. There will have been a human, perhaps more than one, who started this whirlpool of pain and death."

"There was a man. They don't like men. They only like women, because a woman released them to die." Satya filled in.

Chloe shuddered. "That's..."

"Vile," Mr. Crour filled in. "Miss Brandt, are you certain you want or need to know more?"

"Just one thing. When they... when the police dig them up, will they be..."

"At rest. At rest at last." Satya sounded further away. "Found graves, found homes. Good night..." His voice faded away into nothingness.

"I think that is our cue, Miss Brandt. The night is growing chill, and I asked Della to have cocoa ready against our return."

Chloe shivered. She hadn't been cold until he mentioned it.

They made their way carefully back to the road. Neither of them spoke, until Chloe started the utility vehicle and the headlights breached the darkness. Clouds had come in, and not even the stars gave them light now.

"Won't the police want to know why things like this keep happening in Belleview?" Chloe asked, turning to look at her boss's face in the faint light reflected from the lights. He regarded her, his eyes in shadow.

"I think, Miss Brandt, that you will find there is no mention of Belleview at all in the media." Which wasn't an answer.

"But won't the *police* be suspicious?" She pushed him.

"I have never asked." He made a gesture. "Cocoa, Miss Brandt. Worry about the world outside the cemetery later. For tonight, the mysteries are solved and the curtain has fallen on our little drama. The stage is left to the outsiders, for the morrow."

"Was that Shakespeare?" she asked, setting them in motion.

"Good heavens! What did they teach you at that school?" He laughed. "I see I need to add to your lessons."

"*Oh, nooo!*" She joined him in laughing.

The door opened when they pulled up, warm yellow light spilling out. Chloe hurried up the steps, Mr. Crour behind her, and greeted Della cheerfully.

"Oh, cocoa and food! I'm starving!" She stopped. "I could hug you!"

The skeleton lifted one hand to her rows of pearly teeth, and Chloe thought there was a twinkle in the depths of her eye sockets.

"Not done, but she appreciates the sentiment very much." Mr. Crour said from behind her, closing the door on the night. "Now, let me introduce you to the magic of vinyl..."

They talked a little, but mostly, listened to recordings of what Mr. Crour called 'old Bill' irreverently, while they ate and drank. Chloe felt a weight lift off her, and saw her boss as relaxed as she could ever remember seeing him. It seemed like he was right. They had done what they could. There would be time tomorrow for more worry and care. Today, they had kept their ends up and done their job.

"You should come tomorrow and see my snake play dead, sir."

"I'd like that very much, Miss Brandt."

"Goodnight."

"Sleep well."

About the Author

Cedar Sanderson is an author, artist, and scientist. She has fourteen novels in print, and numberless shorter works, she can't keep track of them all. She lives in northern Texas with her husband and a cat named Lightly Toasted Marshmallow. You can find her art, fiction snips, and recipes at www.cedarwrites.com.

ALSO BY CEDAR SANDERSON

ALSO IN THIS SERIES:

The Groundskeeper: Raking up the Dead

The Groundskeeper: The Hoodoo that You Do

The Groundskeeper: My Ghoul

The Groundskeeper: Deadhead

SLIGHTLY CONNECTED:

Lab Gremlins

Possum Creek Massacre

OTHER SERIES BY CEDAR SANDERSON:

Pixie Noir

Three books set both in our world and Underhill

Vulcan's Kittens

A young adult duology enjoyed by readers of all ages

Tanager's Fledglings

The first two books in a space opera trilogy, book three will be released soon!

AND NOW FOR SOMETHING REALLY DIFFERENT:

Running Into Time

The Case of the Perambulating Hatrack

YOU MIGHT ALSO LIKE...

DUST OF THE OCEAN

By Dorothy Grant

In the ruins of an ancient alien city, a half-alien slave's act of mercy will change the course of a cold war.

When Mika saves Arkady, a wounded enemy soldier, he offers her a path to freedom. All it will take is finding a hidden artifact that may alter the course of an interstellar conflict...

But the path there will plunge their team into the depths of inhuman nightmares, battling ancient bioweapons and outwitting her former owners. It's going to take everything they have just to survive, much less escape with their prize!

FAMILIAR TALES

By Alma Boykin

Welcome to a world where Familiars choose magic

workers, and a few others, as their partners. A world of adventure, tax-deductions, bad publisher tricks, and odd veterinary clinics, where wolverines wear glasses and iguanas sing along with the radio—badly—while casting spells and keeping their chosen humans out of mischief.

Or try to.

RIMWORLD: INTO THE GREEN

By J.L. Curtis

After a chance encounter with Dragoons and Traders turns a routine planet exploration into a rout that kills his team and his career, Lieutenant Ethan Fargo, medically retired, wants nothing more than to hole up in the backwater Rimworld he'd explored and enjoy a quiet retirement far from people or problems.

Unfortunately, he's about to find out that he's not as retired as he wants to be, and that his new home system comes with dangers, politics, and Dragoon sightings of its own. What promised to be a boring retirement will turn out to be anything but.

STAND ALONE (WOLFHOUNDS BOOK 1)

By John Van Stry

Chase had it all planned out, do a little time in one of the emperor's jails, say a four year stretch for getting rid of some trash that no one would miss, and when he got out, the path to the leadership would be wide open. It wasn't enough to be one of the gang's rising stars, or better lieutenants, he needed jail time, serious jail time — not that juvie crap or just going to county, to garner the respect he needed and deserved.

Unfortunately his bastard of a father, the same one that left his mother to die in poverty and him to run wild on the streets took an interest. Seeing him sitting on the bench when his case went to court was a shock. But not as big a shock as being sentenced to ten years in the Imperial Navy.

CECIL THE COMBAT WOMBAT

By Kelly Grayson

He didn't ask for cartilaginous ass plates, but military science made him a warrior. And late at night when the nightmares come of innocents killed or twerking an enemy to death in a dark tunnel, he tells himself he did it to protect the other wombats in his unit. He sucks it up, soldiers on and does his duty.

He's Cecil the Combat Wombat, and he's seen some shit, man.

Made in the USA
Coppell, TX
21 January 2026